EVE AINSWORTH

To all the Dick Kerr Ladies throughout the years.
May your stories never stop being told.

With thanks to Gail Newsham, official archivist of the Dick, Kerr Ladies football team.

Dick, Kerr Girls Kicking Off is a uclanpublishing book

First published in Great Britain in 2020 by
uclanpublishing
University of Central Lancashire
Preston, PR1 2HE, UK

First published in theUK 2020

978-19129792-0-2

1 3 5 7 9 10 8 6 4 2

Set in 11.5/18pt Kingfisher by Amy Cooper

A CIP catalogue record for this book is available from the British Library.

Printed and bound in Great Britain by Clays Ltd, Elcograf S.p.A.

FOREWORD

When I was at primary school, I liked to play football. I was what my parents called a 'tomboy' – I liked to climb trees and make stuff and read adventure books – but at school, I wasn't allowed to play football because it was 'a boys' game'. In PE, us girls had to play netball instead, which somehow didn't seem half so much fun. Sometimes, though, the boys would let me play football with them, but I was usually in goal because nobody else wanted to be goalie. 'You're quite good, for a girl,' they told me.

Things may have changed a little now, but too slowly. These days, as an author, I still get emails and letters from girls asking if I'll ever write about football, because they love it. I don't think I'll ever write a book about football, but I've fallen in love with this one. It tells a story of courage in the face of adversity, of overcoming the odds and smashing the barriers that barred women from football . . . and it's full of heart and warmth and hope.

And it isn't fiction . . . Way back at the end of World War One, women and girls were pushing the boundaries and proving that they could be every bit as good as men on the footy field. Awesome, right? This really happened, and author Eve Ainsworth has woven the story of a football team made up of factory girls into a gripping, heart-warming story.

Reading *Kicking Off*, I was transported back in time to an age when a fifteen-year-old girl could be called up to work in a munitions factory, standing all day at a production line, handling dangerous explosives . . . a time when Britain was at war and every family had someone fighting at the front, or had lost somebody in battle. This is a story of friendship, family and football, and I think you're going to love it.

Cathy Cassidy

It was October 1917 when my life truly changed.

I suppose that's quite a flippant thing to say, really, when our country was already fighting a war that many of us privately worried we'd never be able to win. Families all around were struggling. The future, if you could ever bring yourself to think about that, looked bleak for most of us. But the truth is – without the war, who knows where I may have ended up? Without the war, who knows who I might've become. Of course, I should never be thankful that such a cruel and awful event happened, but I am thankful for what that time did for me and my life, as well as for many other girls like me.

I really think, that in many ways, it was the making of us.

For us, it was a new beginning.

When I was called up to help in the war effort – a gangly fifteen-year-old with frizzy hair and barely a sensible thought in my head – I wasn't as frantic as some girls

I knew. I didn't cry, or try to convince my doctor that I had some rare disease that would stop me working. I didn't know what to expect; I simply accepted my fate and tried to make the best of it. Worries (as Mam had drilled into me) were best ignored, they only caused more trouble.

I found out I was to become a factory worker, building the weapons that our brave soldiers would use on the front line. I had little say in the matter, even though I had no real idea what this work would involve. It wasn't like I could protest or ask to do something else. This was to be my assignment now. At least, like Dad said, I wasn't to be facing 'God knows what in some far-off land'.

I'd seen the posters they'd put up in the street. Special ones addressed to us girls. One had stopped me dead in my tracks. I took a moment to stop and read it twice, to really take in the message.

ON HER
THEIR LIVES DEPEND

It was just there, glued up on the fence opposite our street. You couldn't miss it. I had been walking back from the shop and I ended up frozen on the spot, staring up at it. Something inside me stirred and I had to hug my coat close to my body to stop myself from shivering, even though I was still clutching the loaf of bread I had just bought for Mam. I had to read the words again, this time out loud.

'. . . lives depend . . .'

It made me shiver again.

'On her . . . lives depend.'

On her . . .

The country needed women.

It needed me.

I suppose that meant I counted for something too.

Of course, there were other posters all over town, all promoting the war effort. They had been up for ages now – ripped and weather-worn, but seen by thousands. They had been there to remind men of their duty, in case they ever dared to forget it. It was a similar poster to this one that my big brother Freddie had seen in town all those months ago, one that told him that his country needed him. After reading that, he had come home with a sudden determined energy.

'I have to go and fight, Hettie,' he said. 'I can't just sit around while men are dying. I have to play my part.'

It didn't matter, he said, that he was only sixteen. It didn't matter that Mam cried and cried and told him he was too young, or that Dad stopped talking to him for days, locked in a darker mood than ever before. Freddie had decided that he was old enough to be part of something important. He needed to do his bit. His mind was made up.

I knew he was scared, though. This was my Freddie after all. Lovely, gentle Freddie. He wasn't a fighter. That wasn't him. Freddie dreamt of stopping work at the factory one day and learning to become a photographer. He wanted to go to far-away places.

'I'll be all right,' he told me, brushing my cheek with a cool kiss. 'I'll be home soon. I promise.'

And so, we watched him, and others like him, leaving for war. Leaving for a dark, brutal, unknown world that we'd only heard rumours about. Dad wasn't there, of course, he was busy at work, but I think even if he hadn't been, he wouldn't have wanted to go and see Freddie off. Dad didn't talk much about his views on it all, but I knew he didn't agree with war and he didn't like the idea of his only son going away to be part of one.

'It's killing for killing's sake,' he would mutter under his breath. 'Lives lost, and for who? Someone tell me who we are fighting for, because it's not for the likes of us.'

His views were not popular ones. Even Mam scolded him for being unpatriotic and cold. She said he should be there to see his boy leave.

The trams were leaving for the train station from the early morning until late at night and it was quite a sight to see. All of these young men, jostled together, ready to join their fellow soldiers already out there fighting. They didn't seem scared at all – in fact, most of them were laughing and joking and singing songs at the top of their voices. I would have been shaking like a leaf. My last sight of Freddie was of him standing at the back of the long line, looking so smart and tall in his khaki uniform. He saw me and Mam standing there, and he winked at us. That was his way of saying, 'I'll be all right. You don't need to worry.'

But of course, Mam did worry. Especially when the old lady next to us shook her head sadly and said, 'You know most of these poor lads won't make it back.'

I'd never seen Mam so angry. She flashed the woman one of her coldest stares and snapped back, '*My* boy will be back. He's a fighter. He's doing what's expected of him.'

Because that's what the men did of course – what was expected of them. They sorted out all the problems while us women sat at home, waiting and praying and keeping the house clean for their return. I'd often wondered if that was enough, really. The suffragettes round our way certainly didn't think so. They had been going on for ages now, demanding that women should be treated differently

– *equally*. Dad just got angry at the mere mention of them. He said they were 'daft women that needed their heads sorting out'.

Mam didn't say much about it, though. She looked at Dad with a tired, sad sort of expression and simply shook her head. I'd heard her talking to our neighbour, Edna Jones, about Edith Rigby. She was a Preston lass who was well known for her local suffragette activities – most famously for burning Lord Leverhulme's home in Rivington. Dad called Edith a 'dangerous and crazy woman' with ideas above her station, but when I listened to Mam talking, I heard her using the words 'brave' and 'strong-willed', which made my ears prick up. I thought Edith Rigby sounded rather wonderful, and not daft at all.

Now, with the war raging on, women would have to be brave. We were being called up too. Here was the evidence – with this poster, with my new job.

We could help. We could fill the space that the men had left. We could creep into the shadows and the gaps and quietly take over where they had left off. And maybe we could even be as good as men – just like Edith had been saying. We could make a difference.

So that poster, that simple sheet of tatty paper, nailed to the fence and torn slightly at the corner, helped me make to make sense of one of the most important things I'd ever had to do.

What I didn't know right then, was that this would be something that would change my life for ever.

I lived on Spa Road, a small street off Marsh Lane – which itself branched off the long Strand Road where the huge Dick, Kerr & Company Factory stood. This would now be my place of work for as long as they needed me. I wasn't quite sure what would be involved, but I knew that I would be helping to fill the munitions shells that would be used for the war. If I was honest, it all sounded a bit dangerous and I was worried about handling explosive chemicals, but I didn't want to say anything for fear of looking cowardly. I knew from Freddie a little of what life was like at the factory. Freddie had been an apprentice there himself, working with the draughtsmen. He'd already seen some of the women start working there before he left himself.

'They call them canaries,' he'd said. 'That's because their skin can get a yellow glow from the TNT that they have to work with. They have to pack it into the shells, you see; it's mucky work. Not easy at all.'

'Their skin really turns yellow?' I'd asked.

'Well, yes – over time. Even their hair can turn a strange yellow colour.'

'That can't be good for them,' I'd said, shocked.

Freddie had shrugged. 'Who knows? But what they're doing is important – they can't be worrying about anything else when there's a war to win.'

'Isn't TNT an explosive?' I'd asked, then.

'Oh, yes. It's mighty dangerous. There was one time when a shell exploded in the factory. The poor lass that was working with it was only eighteen or so. She lost two fingers.'

At the time, I'd tried to hold back my disgust – I didn't want Freddie to think I was silly or weak – but now, *I* was going to be one of those women. Despite my nerves, I was convinced I was doing the right thing. If I became a canary – so be it. At least I wouldn't be alone.

Freddie told me all about the Dick, Kerr Factory not knowing that I would one day be part of it. He, like so many men that lived in the area, had sought work from this great industrial giant. Even our own Dad had worked there for a time, long ago, before moving on to his back-breaking job on the docks.

Dick, Kerr was part of us all, our community – it was part of our identity. Everyone always knew someone who worked there. We were used to the sight of the big, bulky building and we were all used to the thick fumes that pumped into the air. It had always been a great beast of a factory, making trams and lighting, and it was even responsible for the electrification of the railway from Liverpool to Southport. Everyone from these parts was proud of Dick, Kerr and what it had achieved.

Freddie used to make me laugh, telling tales about the loud, bawdy men who worked there. He even told me about the football they would play at breaktime and lunchtime and how rubbish most of the men were at it.

'You'd think they'd never touched a ball before,' Freddie would complain. 'I mean, I'm not much better, but at least I can kick the ball properly.'

Most of all, Freddie talked about Alfred Frankland, who also worked at the factory as a draughtsman and was, in Freddie's eyes, a man of incredible warmth and intelligence. He was the man to whom Freddie had confessed his dream of becoming a photographer, and unlike Dad, Mr Frankland hadn't scoffed or bitten back with cruel words – instead, he suggested Freddie start saving towards his first camera.

Yet now, Freddie was in France – and that dream seemed so very far away.

2

I stood outside our small terraced house, looking up at the tiny dark windows. This had always been my home – our home – and I always had a warm feeling inside my belly when I reached our front door and stood on Mam's freshly washed tiled step. Everything was always so safe and familiar. I've never been one to talk about escaping, like our Freddie – in truth I've always been quite settled here in Spa Road, content with my lot. Dreams were for other people. Like Mam once said, 'dreams only lead to disappointment', and it's much more sensible to focus on the here and now and be happy with what you have.

Except, it was hard to feel happy now that our house was so much emptier. Without Freddie's loud voice and long, lean body taking up all the space, everything seemed wrong. It felt like he was the glue that held us all together.

Behind me, I heard a shout which woke me from my troubled thoughts. I turned to see Ronnie and Davey Marshall, the twins that lived a few doors down from us, out on the street. Two little scallywags with scruffy chestnut-coloured hair, freckles scattered on their cheeks and legs so skinny that they looked like they could snap in two.

Ronnie was clutching a very tired-looking football.

'Hey! Hettie! Join us for a kick around?'

I couldn't help but agree. It had always lifted my mood to play with Freddie, before he left. Hitching up my skirt, I ran over to them. Ronnie placed the ball on the cobbled street and guided a pass over to me. I controlled it with my booted foot and then quickly moved down the side of the street, nimbly avoiding Davey's outstretched leg. Spotting Ronnie on my right, I squared a neat pass to him and then watched in satisfaction as he drove the ball between the two bins at number thirty-five – their makeshift goal.

Ronnie ran over to me in glee. 'That were an amazing pass, Hettie.'

'Thanks.' I glowed.

Davey was sulking, his hands planted on his hips. 'I didn't know you'd be that good.'

'Why? Because she's a girl?' Ronnie asked. He grinned broadly. 'I've spotted her playing with her brother. She's pretty good . . .' He hesitated.

'For a girl?' I finished for him.

He shrugged. 'Yeah – for a girl. I mean, it's not like you're *meant* to be good at it, is it?'

I frowned a little. I knew he was right – that was what everyone else thought. But it still didn't stop the frustration inside of me. Why shouldn't a girl be good at football? What on earth was stopping us? At least Freddie never seemed to think like that. He always said I could play as well as anyone else and why should it matter what was between our legs?

That had made me giggle.

'Wanna play again?' Ronnie said brightly.

I nodded. Why not?

Ronnie took the ball and dribbled down the left of the street. He was fast and quick with his feet, especially for a young lad. I moved myself away from Davey (who wasn't quite as fast) and called for the ball. But just as Ronnie lofted it in my direction, I heard someone yelling my name.

I spun round in alarm.

Dad was standing at the end of the street. He must've come home from work early. His face was like thunder.

'Hettie!' he bellowed. 'Stop that, right now.'

I tried to protest but he was already marching in my direction.

'Stop that, right now,' he hissed. 'You're showing yourself up.'

And without another word, he stormed into the house. I knew that was my cue to follow.

'I'm sorry,' I stuttered to the twins.

I should've known better. Dad hated it when attention was drawn to him in any way, hated it when he thought people were judging us.

Sometimes I felt like Dad hated everything about me. I don't know how old I was when I realised there was something not quite right about him. Perhaps my little sister Martha's age – four or five? Doubts began to flutter in my mind when I saw how other fathers acted – Queenie Ross's dad would tell us all jokes in the street and produce magic tricks from his sleeve. He never frowned or complained if we made too much noise in his company, and seemed to like having us around.

'Your dad's in a lot of pain,' Mam would say in hushed tones when Dad wasn't even in the room. 'After the accident, he was never the same.'

'What accident?'

'Never you mind, lassie.'

I still didn't know the full story of what had happened to Dad, long before I was born, but Freddie told me fragments. I found out it involved a tram and Dad drinking far too much, yet again, at the pub. Apparently, he was lucky to only escape injury to his back and legs. It's strange how Dad never seemed like a man who considered himself lucky.

'He still has to work so hard, that's the thing,' Freddie said. 'We still need the money, otherwise we'd end up in trouble. He drinks now to ease the pain. He says nothing else works.' Freddie shrugged. 'There's no point talking to him about it. I think he just copes the best way he can.'

Sometimes, when I was up early and unable to go back to sleep, I would watch Dad through the bedroom door as he left to work on the docks. His back was always stooped over, as if he was bearing a huge weight on his shoulders, and his thick, dark hair was always neatly combed back away from his tired face. His movement was slow and deliberate, each footstep looked as though it was weighed down with stones. I'd always wonder if anything would ever make him happy again.

When my first day of work came, all my bravado and confidence had disappeared. Suddenly I was a nervous little girl again, too scared to leave my own house. Why had I put myself up for this? What was I trying to prove? Like Dad had said, I wasn't the type who could cope with tough factory work. I would probably be a hindrance, not a help. What if I made a mistake, or a nuisance of myself? Would the other girls laugh at me? Would I even fit in?

You'll surprise yourself with what you can do. It'll be easier than you think.

That was what Mam had tried to convince me of, anyway. Mam knew I was doing the right thing. She told me that I needed to think of this as me 'playing my part' and 'making a difference'. Just like Freddie. Except, this wasn't a bit like Freddie, because even the mention of his name made her eyes start to water and she had to stop talking straight away. We all knew that what Freddie was doing was brave and terrifying and courageous. I was simply going to work.

She tipped my head up so that she could examine my face properly. Spitting quickly on her hankie, she roughly swept it across my cheek. I tried not to flinch. That would only make her rub harder. I hated it when she did this.

'You can't show up there looking a state,' she muttered. 'I won't have that lot talking bad about us.'

'Leave her be, Ethel.'

Dad was nestled by the kitchen table, sharpening the kitchen knife on the old worn slate. He barely looked at us as he worked away, but that was normal these days. He didn't have time for idle chatter. He said that was 'wasted breath'. There was no sign at all of Martha. I assumed she was still up in our room, reading her book or drawing one of her pictures. She'd left the kitchen just after breakfast in a particularly quiet mood.

Martha was never one to like being around tension. She may have only been ten, but she was as sharp as any of us. Although she hadn't mentioned Freddie at all, I knew she missed him fiercely, and she didn't like the idea of me leaving for work, either. 'Everything is changing,' she'd said, before slipping out of the room.

I stared up at Mam's face. There was so much that I wanted to say to her. I wanted to tell her how scared I felt about the day ahead, I wanted to tell her how my insides were all rubbery and my legs felt like lead weights.

I'm not ready, Mam, I wanted to say. *Not really. I don't know why I thought I could do this. I'm not like everyone else. I don't want to be inside a loud factory with girls I don't know. I don't even like things being different.*

She was looking at me in that stern way of hers. Her cheeks were already pink from hanging the clothes out in the shared yard. Her eyes were like two dark-grey pools, not giving anything away. I knew she knew I was worried, but she wouldn't want to be caught up in any of my nonsense. She didn't have time for it.

'Don't be late,' she said sharply. 'If you're tardy they will not think good of you. It'll look bad for the rest of the family, and I won't have that.'

I pulled on my thin coat and nodded. Dad still wasn't looking my way. Sometimes I wondered if he ever noticed I was there at all. I could disappear in a puff of smoke and I doubt he would notice. Sadness gripped me and I almost called out to him.

At the door, Mam lightly touched my head. 'It'll be all right,' she said finally. 'You'll see. You might even enjoy it.'

'I hope so, Mam,' I whispered.

The air was sharp and bitter as I stepped outside. I drew my coat closer to my chest and started walking across the cobbles and up the narrow street. I looked back at our tired terraced house. It wasn't all ours, of course. I used to pretend sometimes that we lived in all of it, but that was just fanciful nonsense. We were luckier than most – Mam kept reminding me of that that. Dad's long shifts meant that we could afford to rent our three rooms. At least we weren't in the cold, damp cellar where Mrs Foster lived, with the cough that rattled her chest and the noise that bled through the walls at night.

My legs still felt unsteady and my feet turned clumsily on the cobbles. I could already see other women making their way in the same direction and I followed behind them like a lost sheep.

I listened to the women chatter as we walked down the main street towards the factory gates. It was quite comforting, listening to the familiar rise and fall of their voices. There were two of them walking immediately ahead of me. They looked older than me, maybe by a few years or so, but it was hard to tell from behind. One of the women was particularly tall with long hair swept up away from her face. She had a loud, sparkly laugh which made her seem so confident. The woman beside her was smaller and stockier with dark, wild hair that was cut shorter.

'He doesn't know what he's on about,' the shorter girl said scornfully; her voice was loud and whipped easily in the breeze. 'I bet he wouldn't say that to my face.'

'Mine, neither,' the other woman replied bluntly. 'Bloody men – don't know what they're on about half the time.'

I tried not to listen in, after all, no one likes an earwigger, but it was hard not to get caught up in their conversation.

The shorter woman must have sensed my presence behind them as she suddenly turned to look in my direction. Her face was round and her light brown hair neatly shaped around it. Her large eyes peered at me, not unkindly but certainly with curiosity.

'So . . .' she said. 'Who are you, then, following us?'

I could feel my cheeks blaze under her gaze. 'I'm sorry,' I said, stepping back a bit. 'I'm Hettie Blakeford. I start at the factory today.'

'You're starting today?' She nudged the shorter dark-haired girl, who giggled. 'At Dick, Kerr's? I don't believe you. How old are you?'

'Nearly sixteen,' I muttered, knowing what answer I would get back.

'Sixteen? You look no more than a child! Twelve, at the very least!' she squealed. 'Look, Flo! They're recruiting babies now.'

The taller girl had stopped walking and was looking me up and down in quite a kindly manner. She drew her hand over her hair, as if smoothing it. 'Aw, leave her alone, Alice Kell. You're making her go red all over. She's just dainty, that's all.'

I was going red! I could feel my entire body raging under their gaze. I knew I looked small and frail. Everyone said it, from Dad (who called me the runt of litter) to Mam, who tried to build me up with her disgusting castor oil. Only Freddie told me not to worry. He always said that there were advantages to being small, then he'd wink at me and kiss the top of my head. I loved him for saying it, but I'd not discovered what these so-called advantages were yet and wasn't sure if I ever would.

Alice Kell pursed her lips. Although I think she was trying to look put out, I noticed her eyes were twinkling a little. She looked as though she was full of mischief. I could feel myself begin to relax a little. These women were kind, I could tell.

'Another Dick, Kerr girl, hey?' she said lightly. 'And the smallest one yet! Welcome to the gang, kid!'

'You stick with us, Hettie. We'll look out for you,' Flo added gently.

'Flo Redford looks after everyone, don't you dear?' Alice smiled at her friend. 'Well, welcome lass. Let's get a hurry on. Don't want to be late on your first day now, do we?'

I smiled back. I'd never been part of anything before, let alone a gang. This didn't feel bad at all.

'Ta,' I said back, walking quicker so I was in line with them.

I was pleased to be part of it.

I didn't know then, of course, that this was only just the beginning.

So here I was now, outside the factory where Freddie had once worked. A place that was so familiar to me and yet, in many ways, still so very strange and new.

The Dick, Kerr factory stood proudly on the long Strand Road. It was a dreary-looking building, no more than a two-storey brick warehouse, but somehow it seemed more imposing than that, with its high walls and grim steel-framed windows. I had to catch my breath slightly as I stood outside, my head tipped back to take it all in. I couldn't quite believe this was where I would be spending my time from now on.

We all have to do our bit. Mam's words rattled in my mind. *Times are different now.*

I breathed out hard. They certainly were. Would anything ever be the same again?

'It's quite a sight, ain't it,' Flo said, nudging me. 'You wait till you see inside. It's bloody huge. It's a wonder we don't all get lost.'

'And noisy . . .' muttered Alice, screwing up her nose.

'Mark my words, you'll have a headache by the end of the day. And your ears will be ringing.'

'A whole day stuffing shells,' Flo moaned, staring down at her nails. 'How glamorous can you get?'

'It could be worse, Flo – you could be cleaning the lavvy.'

Both girls giggled. Alice nudged me gently. 'Never mind Flo. She's a bit of a fancy one. Doesn't like getting her nails dirty.'

Flo ruffled her hair as if on cue and then marched through the factory gates, sighing.

'It'll be all right,' Alice said to me kindly. 'You'll soon find your feet, and the girls aren't so bad once you get to know them a bit.' She winked. 'In fact, most of them aren't bad at all.'

We walked across the yard towards the large main doors. I immediately noticed a young lad, possibly a bit younger than me, who was kicking a tatty-looking ball against the wall as we passed. His shot was very awkward. I paused for a moment, compelled to watch him. A tingle of memory sparkled within me.

'Ey, George! There's no time for that now!' Alice shouted over to him.

The lad, George, stuck his tongue out at her. He had bright pink cheeks and messy dark curls that spilled over his forehead. 'Need to get my practice in, don't I?' he said back brightly. 'Won't get a chance later.'

'You'll need more practice if you keep scuffing it like that, lad,' Flo shouted back.

George frowned. 'And what would you know about it?'

Flo turned round to face us, one eyebrow raised. She really was quite beautiful. I had difficulty looking at her directly; I suddenly felt quite shy.

She placed one hand on her chest, feigning horror. 'Oh – what would I know? I am but a woman, after all.' She fluttered her eyelashes at me and Alice and we both sniggered. 'I couldn't possibly kick a ball with my delicate feet,' she continued. 'Or run around a dirty pitch. What would happen to my hair?'

'Women can't play sport – you know that,' George scoffed. 'You'd look daft.'

'Heaven forbid,' Alice said, more stoutly. 'What a thought! The world would stop spinning, I'm sure, if such a thing were to happen.'

George was red-faced by now, standing with his hands firmly placed on his hips. 'You might laugh,' he said. 'But women are not made to play football. It's just how it is.'

Flo nudged me. 'It's just how it is, apparently? Who knew? I'd better give my football boots to charity.'

'Do you play, then?' I asked her, amazement swirling in my belly. It was all I could do not to grin at her like a complete idiot.

Flo smiled back at me. 'Well, you'd think not, according to smarty-pants over there, but yes, I play sometimes, and so does Alice. Why, do you?'

I could feel myself turn red again. I hated the way I blushed at everything. 'Oh, not really,' I stammered. 'My brother used to play and I used to watch him a bit. I liked to mess around. I'm not very good.'

Alice smiled. 'Well, you're not alone, you'll find a few girls here that like to mess around with a ball. And quite a few of them are not at all half-bad.' She shot a look towards George. 'Despite what others might say.'

George muttered something under his breath, picked up his ball and stalked off. I didn't much like the look he shot us before he moved away, though. It was a glare of pure loathing.

'Never mind him,' Flo said, nudging me gently. 'He's just a bit mardy. You need to watch out though – now Alice has got wind that you like football, she'll be on at you about it all day long.'

Alice shook her head. 'I won't be doing anything of the sort. Not any more. I can't be bothered with that lark now. There's no point.' She smiled sadly at me. 'A few of the girls here are good with the ball – that's all. And a few others are jealous of that fact.'

'You'd make a proper decent player, Alice, if you gave it a chance,' Flo said smoothly. 'Strong lass like you. If you're anything like your brothers, you'd be better than most.'

'Can we not talk about this now!' Alice barked back.

Flo held her hands up in defence. 'Eh, I'm sorry Alice. I wasn't thinking. Ignore me.'

I shuffled my feet and looked down at the floor – this was clearly something private between the two girls.

'It's fine, Flo,' Alice said softly. 'I'm just not in the right mind to be thinking about football again. Not so soon after Tom.' She paused. 'You're a fine one to talk, anyway. I've seen you messing with the ball. You're as good as any of us.'

Flo grinned. 'I told you I might give it a proper go one day. If we ever had an actual team. Which of course will never happen, not with the likes of George around, putting us down at every turn. It's true I'm used to mucking about at home, but I'm not sure it'll be the same here.'

'Grace reckons it would, given half the chance,' Alice said.

'Well, it's hardly likely, is it? Girls have only just

been allowed on to the factory floor, never mind the football pitch.' Flo laughed. 'They wouldn't want us to get carried away.'

'Who's Grace?' I asked.

Flo grinned. 'Ah, you'll meet her soon enough, I'm sure. Let's just say – if you think I like football, Grace is on another level.'

'Aye,' Alice agreed. 'If anyone can change things around here, it's our Grace.'

I nodded slowly, but inside I felt sad. Surely Flo and Alice were kidding themselves. They knew women weren't meant to like that sort of thing. Not football. Everyone knew that. Apart from Freddie, that is.

Freddie was mad about football and, when I was old enough, he'd let me join in with him. Of course, I was rubbish to begin with, kept tripping over my own feet. It didn't help that Dad would often be watching from the back door, shouting at Freddie for wasting his time with me. Freddie never really listened to Dad though. He would whisper under his breath that Dad was old-fashioned.

'The world is changing,' he'd said firmly one evening, not long before he left for France. 'We have to learn to change with it.'

Over time, Freddie had begun to take it more seriously

with me. He told me that if I was going to learn to play, I should do it properly. He used to make me run up and down with the ball in the street, wearing a pair of his old football shoes and an extra pair of socks to hold them on tight. He'd place old tin cans up the path for me to control and dribble the ball around, like it was glued to my feet.

I loved those times together. At first, just because I loved being around Freddie. But then it became clear that I loved spending time with the ball too. It was hard work but enjoyable too. And I was good at it.

I was *actually* good at something.

But then Freddie left us and everything changed.

Inside the factory was an explosion of noise. It took me a moment or two to get a handle on my senses because it was just so overwhelming. There were workbenches spanning the entire length of the cavernous space. Machines roared and hissed. Even over the noise of the machines, I could hear the sound of laughter and loud chatter lighting up the room.

We had already hung up our coats and bags in the cloakroom and were dressed in our white aprons and hats. Alice had already rushed off to her station, muttering under her breath about 'not wanting to be told off for being late'. Flo stayed with me, though, and smiled kindly at me, like she knew I was worried.

'It's not too bad,' she said, 'once you get the hang of it. You can always come and find me if you need to.'

I immediately began to relax a little. I liked Flo Redford a lot. It was so kind of her to take the time to make sure I was OK. And I wished I could look as glamorous as she did in her uniform. I noticed how the few boys in the room couldn't take their eyes off her as she passed them by.

'I'm sorry about the talk earlier,' she added as we walked. 'I shouldn't have gone on at Alice about football. It was wrong of me. She's still very upset.'

'Why?' I asked. 'Did something happen?'

Flo's voice dropped further. 'She lost her brother a month or so ago, young Tom. Killed in action. She used to play football with him all the time, so I suppose the memory hurts too much.'

'That's so sad,' I said.

'Isn't it? They were very close. I don't think she's been the same for a while.'

Flo walked me over to the supervisor, a tall elderly man with a sprig of ginger hair. He glared down at me as if he'd never seen my like before.

'This is Hettie. She's new,' Flo explained to him. 'Starts today, so be a bit kind, eh?'

'Oh, she is, is she?' he barked back, as if I wasn't there.

'This is Mr Reid,' Flo said brightly. 'Pay no attention to him, his bark is worse than his bite.'

Mr Reid's top lip curled. He certainly looked a bit like the bulldog that lived on the corner of our street. 'You get back to work, Miss Redford,' he said bluntly. 'I'll have none of your lip this morning, thank you.'

'Over there is the manager,' Flo said, ignoring Mr Reid, 'Mr Connor. He's not often on the shop floor, he's usually locked away in his office, but when he does come down, he's nice enough.'

I glanced over at the man standing by the main doors across the way. He was short and stocky, with bright silver hair. Mr Connor was chatting to a tallish man who was very smartly dressed, with a small thatch of dark hair on his head. As I stared at them, the taller man looked over in our direction and smiled widely.

'That's Mr Frankland,' Flo said. 'I'm not sure what he does. I think he works in another area. I was also told that he's involved in the sports and social club here.'

I thought of how Freddie had spoken of Mr Frankland in the past and immediately felt a warm glow inside of me. It was like I had something to connect me to Freddie again.

'He's a draughtsman,' I said. 'He worked with my brother, before.'

'Oh, there you go – you see. A familiar face. Now, that's nice, isn't it?'

Mr Connor was also looking over, but there was no smile from him. In fact, he looked quite stern.

'Don't fret, he likes me,' Flo said, waving in his direction. 'But then, I do work extremely hard.'

'I don't see much evidence of that right now, Miss Redford!' Mr Reid barked.

Flo grinned at me. 'Good luck, Hettie,' she whispered, before blowing Mr Reid a kiss and scuttling off.

I stared after her, my insides churning up again, and when I looked back at Mr Reid's stern face I didn't feel much better.

In fact, I felt bloody miserable.

Mr Reid left me under the instruction of an older lady called Jenny. He said she would be able to show me the ropes and get me working in no time. Jenny, a large woman with a red, scowling face, didn't seem very impressed to have me working beside her.

'You're just a slip of a girl,' she complained. 'Are we recruiting babies now? Eh?'

'I'm nearly sixteen,' I muttered, feeling my cheeks blush.

She sniffed. 'Well, whatever age you are, you need to have your wits about you and concentrate. There's no time to daydream or muck about. Look around you – all the other women are working very hard. They may talk among themselves, but they never take their eyes off the task.'

I nodded to show I understood. Inside, my stomach was twisting itself almost inside out. I was frightened that I might be sick at any moment.

'You need to keep your eye on the task,' Jenny continued brightly. 'We can't afford any slip-ups. Now, just checking – you're not wearing any nylon or silk, are you?'

I shook my head. I had been told in advance not to wear such fabrics, or any jewellery at all (not that I had the pleasure of owning any, anyway).

'Good. Or else, one spark and you'll go up like a flippin' rocket.'

I swallowed hard – I could taste my breakfast rising up from my stomach. Jenny snorted beside me.

'Aye, lass! You already look canary yellow and you've not even started yet. Just watch what I do, all right? It's easy once you know how. As long as you concentrate and take care, you'll be fine.'

She then proceeded to show me how to ram the TNT carefully but quickly into the munition shell. 'Be careful not to spill any, do you see? Slowly does it. And mind how you place the detonator on the top. You have to tap it down in place. Like this, see . . .'

She demonstrated how to quickly lower the detonator into the powder, settling it down with caution.

'Don't rush it,' she warned. 'And don't tap too hard, or the whole thing will go up. You wouldn't want to lose that pretty nose of yours, would you.'

My hands immediately leapt up to my face. 'No. No, I . . .'

'Well, you won't if you're careful,' she said firmly. 'We've not had anyone lose a body part for a while, and I don't want it happening on my watch.'

'I . . .' I hesitated, unsure if I could say it. 'I–I don't know if I can do this.'

Jenny turned to face me, hands resting on her hips, her lips pressed together in a thin line.

'You *can* do this,' she said. 'It's not easy work, no. Your back will hurt and your fingers will ache, but you *can* do this.'

I shook my head. 'But if I make a mistake . . .?'

'You're doing this for them,' she continued. 'You're doing this for our men. For our country. You can do this. We need you to do this!'

I reached towards the shell that was in front of me. I saw how much my fingers were shaking and my stomach flipped over again.

'But what if I make a mistake?' I repeated.

'You won't,' Jenny said. 'Just believe in yourself, lassie, and you won't.'

I stared back down at the workbench. I still felt so sick and giddy, but Jenny was right. I had to do this. What other choice did I have? I couldn't run away now. What would Mam think? What would Dad say?

I had to believe I could do it.

I took a deep breath and picked up my first shell.

***

By the time the lunch bell rang, my back was aching and my fingers were cramped. It felt like I had been working non-stop for days on end, rather than the few hours I had been. How did the other women work so easily, and without complaint? I wasn't quite sure how I would be able to do this, day after day, for heaven's knows how long.

At least the fear of explosions had passed as the morning dragged on. I'd got into a routine of stuffing the powder and tapping the tops with just the right pressure. Jenny commented that my tiny fingers were an advantage – they gave me more dexterity – and this had helped to lift my confidence a little.

I followed the women out to the canteen, keen to eat something to fill my growling stomach. I also longed for some fresh air, but the sound of pelting rain against the windows meant that was not going to be possible today.

As I walked into the canteen, my eyes scanned the room for sight of Flo or Alice. My ears were still buzzing from the noise of the machines and I had the beginnings of a headache forming behind my eyes. It was hard to make out anyone in the crowds; there were just so many of us. Women, many older than me, were either queuing up or sat at tables, talking loudly across the room at each other. There were a few men here, too – the ones that were either essential to the work of the factory or were too young or weak to be signed up.

A loud wolf-whistle pierced the room and it startled me. A group of men were standing at the far side, watching a small group of women pass. One of them, a tall, pretty blonde, wiggled her bottom on purpose as she passed.

'You should be so lucky, Billy Jenkins,' she called back and the boys all burst into laughter.

I could feel heat rising to my face. This was so different to anything I had been exposed to before. Our quiet home, my stilted evening conversations with Mam and Dad. By gum – the only boy I had only really known properly was Freddie, and he was my brother!

My stomach gurgled and I rubbed it self-consciously. I wasn't sure how long our lunchbreak was but I certainly didn't want to miss it by standing around gawping, so I made my way towards the dwindling queue. As I stepped forward, a small group of older women came up behind me, obviously just as hungry but even more impatient than me. They began jostling to get ahead.

'What's taking so long?' one of them barked in my direction.

Feeling shy, I said nothing. But then an elbow struck me in the back.

'Hurry up girl, get moving. We've not got long.'

I stared back at them, not clear how they expected me to move when there was a line of bodies in front of me.

'Cat got your tongue, has it?' said the same woman from before. She looked a good few years older than me, but it was hard to tell. Her expression was sullen and her face doughy and almost baby-like. Her hair was blonde, but had a strange yellowish tinge to it. Even the skin under her hair was a similar colour. It was almost as if she had bent forward and dunked the front of her hair in paint. I guessed she was a true 'canary'.

'I can't very well move,' I said quickly.

'Oooh!' The woman turned to her friends and they all giggled. 'Listen to the lassie! Well, I think you can move if I make it so.'

She reached over and shoved me a little. It wasn't much of a push, but it was enough to unbalance me. I ended up being thrown forward and falling awkwardly against the back of the woman in front of me.

'Hey, watch it!'

She turned around to address me. She was a little taller than me, with dark hair combed away from her face. Her bright eyes gleamed in my direction. I guessed she was older than me too, perhaps in her early twenties.

'What's going on?'

Her gaze fell on me and then to the giggling older women. Her forehead creased.

'Peggy? What are you playing at, eh?' she hissed. 'Pushing around little kids now, are we?'

I straightened my back. 'I'm not actually that little–'

She held out her hand. 'Peggy should know better. She's always in such a hurry to get to the front of the queue, she forgets her manners. Don't you, Peg?'

'Aye, Grace,' Peggy muttered. She ducked her head a little. 'I was only messing.'

Grace! My eyes widened. Was this the same Grace that Flo and Alice had been talking about?

'Well, don't be messing around here,' Grace said shortly. She turned back to me. 'But I have to say, you're the smallest one I've seen here yet.'

I nodded slowly. It was amazing how much smaller I could feel in this huge space with all these loud, confident people. How would I ever fit in?

'Don't worry, pet,' Grace said quietly, seeming to read to my mind and smiling at me. 'Stick here with me, I'll keep an eye on you. You'll soon find your feet.'

'Really? You think so?'

She laughed. 'Oh, I can be sure of it.'

Grace asked if I would like to sit with her and I was only too pleased to, even though my skin prickled at the thought. Why would someone like this want to spend time with me? What if I made a complete fool of myself in front of her? I shook off these thoughts and smiled brightly as we walked together across the hall. I liked the fact that all the other women seemed to know and like her, waving and calling out as she passed them by. But the icing on the cake was that Grace took me over to sit with Flo and Alice. I almost squealed with excitement to see them again; luckily I managed to contain myself in time.

'Ey-up!' Flo said kindly. 'You've found our Grace, then?'

Flo was sat back in her seat in a leisurely fashion, her long legs spread out in front of her. She'd obviously finished her lunch but was in no hurry to leave. Alice was still eating but nodded in my direction and shifted up so that I could sit beside her.

'I caught that Peggy Davies trying to be clever,' Grace said, sitting down heavily next to Flo. 'I didn't care for it, so I told her to stop. She really is quite a madam, that one.'

Flo winked at me. 'You've got Grace looking after you now, Hettie. You're going to be just fine.'

Grace smiled back. She wasn't a big girl by any standards, but I could tell she was strong. It was the way that she held herself and the glint in her eye that told me Grace wasn't one to mess with. It felt good to be in her company. Suddenly this huge, loud hall didn't seem as unfriendly any more.

'How was your morning?' Flo asked me kindly.

'It weren't too bad,' I said shyly, averting my gaze. 'My fingers hurt a little . . .'

'Aye, you'll soon get used to that,' Grace said, nestling herself down in her seat. 'This work will toughen you up, if nothing else.' Her gaze fixed on me and I watched as she looked me up and down. 'A little lass like you sure needs toughening up a bit.'

I blushed again and hated myself for it. Why did I have to be so little and skinny? I must have stood out like a sore thumb here.

Alice rested a hand on my shoulder. 'Don't you worry. It won't take long, and then you'll be just like us – won't she, girls?' She looked up at the others.

Grace snorted. 'What's that then? Gobby?'

The girls all broke into laughter and, despite my nerves, I smiled too.

'Eh, Hettie. You remember I told you some of us like

to play football?' Flo said casually. 'Well, Grace is better than any boy, I'd say.'

Grace frowned a little. 'It's not like we get any chance to, though. A few kicks of the ball when the boys here let us.' She took a mouthful of her food and frowned. 'It's not right. It really isn't. We should be allowed to play whenever we want.'

'Aye. It's not fair,' Flo agreed. 'I still reckon you could take on most of the lads here.'

'And you and Alice could, too,' Grace replied stoutly. 'And the other Alice I work next too, Alice Standing. You all could be good players.'

Flo sniffed. 'No one's interested, Grace. That's the problem.'

Alice sat up in her seat beside me. 'That's the entire problem. What's the point bellyaching about it? No one would ever let a group of girls play football, no more than they'd let us vote.'

'They will one day,' Flo said quietly.

'I like your confidence,' Grace said, grinning at her. 'If it weren't for the suffragettes fighting for our rights, no one would even think it would be possible to change things. But I'm sure it is. I'm quite sure . . .'

Her eyes glazed a little as she seemed to drift into her

own thoughts. Alice continued to eat her food, muttering under her breath and Flo simply smiled at them both.

I ate my lunch quietly, not sure what to say. I knew these women were talking out of turn. Everyone knew that football was a man's sport really. It didn't matter if a woman was to enjoy it, or even if they were any good at it, the fact that they *shouldn't* play was never going to change. Dad had told me the same often enough.

Don't you keep playing that game, Hettie. It's unladylike. It's not fitting.

Like it or not, that was how things were.

'What are you thinking, Hettie?' Flo asked suddenly. 'You have a scowl on your face so deep, it may stay there permanently.'

'I was just thinking – all of this talk of football is pointless. They'll never let us play.'

'Who won't?' Alice asked, looking up.

'Men,' I said back quietly, suddenly aware that all their eyes were on me. My cheeks were blazing even more now. 'Men would never let that happen. It's their sport. It always has been. They won't want to give that up.'

Flo sighed. 'Aye – you've got a point there.'

Grace was very silent, until finally she muttered, 'Yes, well – we'll see about that.'

After lunch, we went back into the cloakroom. Flo and Alice were trailing behind, complaining about feeling tired and wanting to go home already, but Grace was striding at full speed. I wanted to be near to her, so I picked up my pace. She took my arm in hers.

'How are you finding it really, then?' she asked. 'I know the work is pretty grim, but you have to make the best of it, don't you?'

I nodded. 'I don't think it's at all that bad.'

'If you ever struggle, you can talk to me, you know?' Grace pulled a face. 'I've been here a while now. I'd like to think I can help a little. I know it can be tough sometimes but there's lots of good things about the place too.'

I smiled shyly. 'Thank you.'

'You know – when I'm nervous, or sad, my mam always sings that daft song from the music halls to make me feel better.' Grace screwed up her face in concentration. 'Now, how does that one go again . . .' She searched for the words. 'Ah yes – pack up your troubles in your old kit bag—'

'And smile, smile, smile,' I finished for her. It was one of Freddie's favourites. He used to sing it often.

'Sometimes singing while you work helps. It really does. It makes the time go faster. Not that any of these women can hold a note.' Grace giggled softly. 'Still, it's better than complaining. We have to make the best of things, don't we? Everyone has a worry. Everyone has someone they are thinking about. Don't you, Hettie?'

'I do. My brother,' I said. 'I worry about him all the time. He's not been gone long.'

Grace stopped walking for a moment and peered at me. Her expression was sad, but also knowing. Like she understood the jumbled and anxious thoughts that were tumbling through my mind. She gently tugged on my arm.

'My husband, Jimmy, is away fighting, too. I haven't had word from him in so long,' Grace said gently. 'The worry never really goes away. It's always there in the back of your mind. But you do get used to it. Sometimes you can even ignore it, if you can find something to distract you enough.'

Even though I'd never had a sweetheart, I could imagine how I would feel if he had gone to war.

'What do you do to distract yourself?' I asked, keen to find a solution to my troubling thoughts about Freddie.

'Oh, I don't know – all sorts.' Grace smiled again.

'But when I'm here, I usually walk around the yard for a bit and get some air. I find it hard being inside for so long. I think I'm happiest when I feel free, when I can feel the wind in my hair. Does that sound silly?'

I shook my head. It didn't at all.

'It's probably why I love football so much,' she continued. 'I can lose myself. I can run. For a brief time, my thoughts are trouble-free.'

I could tell how much Grace meant what she was saying. I wanted to experience that feeling. *It must be so wonderful.*

The cloakroom was already quite full. A few women sat on one side. Some were smoking and chatting. A couple were leaning up against the wall, peering down at a magazine. Along the other side some men were gathered, talking loudly.

'Bloody miserable day, isn't it,' Grace muttered, looking towards the windows. 'Can't even get outside for a bit.'

'Aye. I was just saying the same to Flo,' Alice replied, as they came up behind us.

We all stared out of the long windows that reflected out to the outside area. The rain was pelting down at quite a rate. Grace drew a deep, ragged breath.

'I guess we won't be going out in that, then.' She forced the window open in a defiant manner, her hair bouncing loose in front of her face. 'I still need air in here though. It gets so stuffy. I hate being stuck in.'

'What's up, Grace? Trying to escape already? Surely it's not come to that?'

One the men was calling to us. He was tall with slicked-back reddish hair and a sulky expression on his face.

Grace pulled a face in his direction. 'If only, Harry . . .' Her attention was diverted to the group of men standing behind him. 'What are you doing over there, anyway?'

Harry's grin broadened. 'Just messing around. You know . . .'

I glanced over. I could see now that one of his group was George, the boy that I'd seen in the yard earlier this morning. Along with George, there were four or five other men and by their feet was the same tatty-looking football from before. It was in an even worse state than Freddie's.

'Not much room to play with that thing,' Grace observed dryly. 'You don't want to go and hurt yourself now.'

'Oh, I'm sure we'll cope,' Harry replied coolly.

As if on cue, one of the men skimmed the ball in Harry's direction. It wasn't well placed and instead, the ball skidded across the floor towards me.

Without thinking, I stopped the ball dead with my foot.

Grace was looking at me with the kind of grin that

Freddie used to flash at me when I did something impressive. 'Oh . . .' she said gently. 'That's interesting.'

I kicked the ball away, suddenly feeling exposed and a little embarrassed. 'It was nothing,' I muttered.

I immediately heard Dad's voice in my head, telling me off for bringing attention to myself – doing things that no decent girl should be doing. What was I even thinking? I was at work, not outside in the street with Freddie. What would they all think of me? That I was some kind of show-off? A rough street kid who should know better?

'Not another one,' George groaned. I glanced up at him, confused, but he continued nonetheless. 'What is it with you girls? You get a job in a man's factory and suddenly you start thinking you know how play a man's sport!' He snorted loudly and his little gaggle of male friends sniggered in response. 'I almost feel sorry for you.'

Grace did not seem fazed. She simply straightened her shoulders a little and looked George straight in the eye. Flo drew a breath. 'Here we go,' she muttered. The other women in the room had stopped chatting now. Everyone was interested in this showdown. I even heard someone whisper, 'You shouldn't say that. Not to Grace. She'll not let you forget it.'

'I don't think I can play. I *know* I can play,' she said,

very quietly. I could feel myself glow inside, like a bunch of coals had been set alight inside my stomach. I'd never met anyone quite like Grace Sibbert before.

There was a pause. Just a brief one. Then Harry scoffed, 'OK, Grace, if you say so.'

'Yes, I say so,' she said coolly. 'And I'll prove it. Pass me that tatty thing you dare to call a ball.'

He hesitated for a second and then passed the ball to Grace's booted feet. 'This should be interesting,' he said, turning to his group. 'Let's see what tricks this girl can perform. With any luck, she'll end up flat on her backside.'

The boys sniggered again.

Grace stared at him for a moment and then smiled sweetly. The expression seemed to light up her entire face. Easing up her long skirt slightly she moved the ball to the other side of the cloakroom, opposite the open window.

'I bet you I can drive this ball clear through that gap,' she said.

Harry shrugged. 'You can try. That's some distance, lass. It's not as easy as it looks. You'll need some loft on that ball.' He sniffed. 'I'd like to see you try.'

'Do you think I can do it?'

At first I thought Grace was asking Harry but when I turned my head to face her, I saw she was looking directly at us. Alice immediately slapped her on the back. 'Of course you can, Gracie!'

Flo simply shrugged. 'I don't doubt it for a second, love.'

Grace's eyes fell on me. 'Do you think I can do it, Hettie?'

I hesitated, stunned that she had even bothered to ask my opinion. Her stare was intense; it was as if my answer really mattered to her.

'Yes,' I said firmly. 'I think you can.'

Grace grinned at me and then turned back to Harry. 'See – that gives me faith now. The new girl believes me. She thinks I can do it.' She positioned herself carefully over the ball. 'Watch yourself, Harry – I think you're going to be eating those words of yours.'

With barely any effort at all, Grace lofted the ball into the air. It swung up and almost seemed to hang, mid-flight, for a few seconds, as if taunting us. From where I was standing, I could already make out its gentle curve as it moved seamlessly through the air, towards the window. It flew through the gap without even touching the frame.

It was a perfect shot.

Something inside of me soared.

Grace stood with her hands firmly on her hips. She sniffed with satisfaction. 'There. It were easy. And I was wearing my work boots too.'

'It was fluke, nowt else,' George shot back, but I could tell he was rattled. He was still staring at the open window like he couldn't believe what had just happened. 'Billy, go fetch that ball back before we lose it for good.'

'Your turn, George,' Grace said, when Billy had passed the ball back to him.

George grinned in response. 'It's easy,' he muttered, and without another word he eased the ball up and through the window. 'See!'

'I bet you us girls can score more shots than you lot,' Grace replied suddenly. Alice giggled next to her.

George stood up straighter. 'You're on! What do you wanna wager?'

Alice stepped forward and reached for his pocket. She took out a small bar of chocolate and gently shook it at him. 'If you win, we'll buy you another bar,' she said smoothly.

'Sounds good,' Harry replied.

'And if we win – you can buy us some Five Boys chocolate,' Alice continued, her eyes still fixed on him. 'Enough for each of us.'

George scoffed. 'Fair enough – but I tell you now, that ain't going to happen.'

'First one to miss, loses,' Grace said sharply. 'Let's do this.'

There was an excited murmuring in the room – suddenly no one was bothered about the rain outside or the impending afternoon shift. All eyes were fixed on this small group in the middle of the factory.

Alice was next to take the ball. She didn't seem nervous at all, as she placed it in front of her feet and then carefully, almost delicately, curled it through the gap. All the women in the room squealed with joy.

'Fluke,' George muttered, but I could see he was worried. Even the lads behind him looked nervous. One of them had started clapping Alice's impressive shot, but stopped when he saw George's stern expression.

'Your turn,' Grace barked. 'Come on. Show us what you're made of.'

The next lad to come to the ball was a tall nervous-looking boy with closely cut black hair. He looked very young, probably younger than me.

'Charlie is our best forward,' George said proudly.

We watched as Charlie positioned the ball on the floor. His cheeks were blazing red and I noticed that he was avoiding all eye contact with us girls.

'Come on, Charlie!' George roared, just as Charlie connected with the ball. Maybe it was the shout that put Charlie off, or perhaps it was nerves, but the poor lad completely scuffed the shot and the ball slammed against the brick wall instead.

The girls roared with excitement. George threw his hat down on the floor in disgust.

'Charlie – what were you thinking? Can you even see straight?'

'I'm quite looking forward to my chocolate later,' Grace said brightly. 'And make sure you get us plenty, George. Enough for each of us, remember?'

We all yelled in agreement.

'You should join us lot for our game tonight,' one of the men in the group said, moving forward. He was larger and rounder than the rest, with a plump face. 'You'll do better than George. He's missed three sitters for us in a row now.'

George turned to the man in fury. 'I never did,' he hissed. 'You needn't be encouraging her, either. Her head will be getting so big soon, she won't be able to fit in this room.'

'I'm not the only girl that can play – there are others, you know,' Grace said matter-of-factly. 'Flo here can too, and there are plenty of others. We could give you a run for your money, any day of the week.'

George snorted. 'Do me a favour. You couldn't play a real sport. This is just messing around – you lot couldn't handle the real thing.'

Grace shrugged. 'If you say so.'

'Tonight, we have a proper match. A real game. You'll soon hear how good we are.'

Grace's smile hadn't slipped at all. 'Maybe. You can tell us all about it tomorrow, George. I'm sure we'd all love to know how you got on.'

The girls murmured in agreement and I found myself nodding along. I was suddenly very keen to hear how the boys played. How wonderful it would be if they were made to look daft again.

The bell echoed around the room for end of lunch, and suddenly there was a scurry of activity as everyone gathered their bits together and prepared to go back to work. Grace tidied up her hair a little and smoothed down her dress. She seemed totally unfazed by what had just happened. Flo was smiling over at Charlie. I guessed she might feel a bit sorry for him.

'You were both amazing just then,' I told Grace and Alice.

Grace giggled. 'Do you think so? Some of the other girls scold me for showing off. But I can't help it.' She dipped her head slightly.

Alice frowned. 'You're not showing off, Grace. You're just showing the men that we can be good at something too. It makes me cross that they think I can't play football as well as they can. I'm as good as any one of those lads, I'd wager.'

Flo tugged on Alice's arm. 'C'mon girl, we'd better hurry; that bell has gone. We don't want to be in trouble for being late.'

Alice nodded in agreement. 'You coming, you two?' she said to me and Grace.

'I will – you go ahead,' Grace said, as the others ran towards the shop floor.

I turned towards her. Her gaze was fixed on the open window, a tiny smile still etched on her face.

'Are you all right, Grace?' I asked.

She slowly moved to face me. 'Oh yes, I'm all right, Hettie. I'm quite all right.' She reached out and lightly touched my arm. 'Tell me. Did you think what we did back there was foolish Do you think it's daft to even try taking on the boys?'

I hesitated. I wasn't really sure how to answer but, looking at Grace's wide stare, I knew I had to be honest. I swallowed hard.

'I don't know, Grace. I mean, this was just high jinks, wasn't it? Nothing serious . . .'

'But what if it were to be serious?' she mused. 'What if we could really show those boys what we could do?'

I shook my head slowly. 'Grace, that would never happen. People wouldn't let you. You know what they say about women doing men's jobs. There's already so much anger out there. People don't like girls doing things above their stations.'

'But it's not above our stations. It's already happening. Other women have set up teams. They're doing it already.' Grace peered at me. 'I can tell you're nervous, Hettie, but isn't there something in you that wants to fight against this – all of this?' She held up her arms and spread them wide. 'You're so young; younger than me. You can be part of the change.'

'I–I want to, but I don't think I can.'

Grace's hard stare fixed on mine. 'Hettie, you can do whatever you want. You just have to believe in yourself.'

I lifted my chin a little, trying to fight the wobble in my voice. 'That's what my Freddie used to tell me.'

Used to... The hollow feeling in my stomach was back.

Grace took my arm. 'Then listen to him. Listen to me. Things can be different, Hettie. I just know it.'

We walked back to the shop floor in silence. The large room was so bright. The noise of the machinery was starting up again. At first I thought that the churning feeling inside my stomach was because of the worry about going back to work. But then I realised that I wasn't worried. I was excited.

Grace was exciting. And so were Flo and Alice.

'I want to believe you, Grace. I do,' I whispered, as I watched Grace retreat to her workstation.

I didn't realise it then, but I'd already met my first proper heroine.

I still talked to him, to my Freddie. They'd all think I was daft if they knew, but I spoke to him as if he were still here with me. His bed was made up in our small cluttered room and I liked to sit on the end of it and pretend that he was there, his head buried under the pillow, moaning at me to stop talking. I could still smell the faint scent of his soap, if I concentrated hard enough, and the stale smell of the socks that he would always wear for too long and then kick under the bed and forget about.

We always used to do this, me and Freddie – talk at night. I'd often slip into our bedroom once he'd finished work and he'd tell me about his day or something funny that one of the lads had said to him. We'd always have to speak in whispers so as not to wake Martha, who would be snoring softly in the next bed. It never crossed my mind that in years to come, I'd be working in the same place that he did. Now I understood why he was always so tired. Why he longed to flop on his bed, stretch out his long legs and let the madness of the day pass over him. Why, some days, he didn't want to talk at all.

Now, I was sat looking at the empty space on Freddie's side of the room. His bed was pushed aside along one wall, looking empty and cold. A pair of his shoes were on the floor at the foot of the bed, as if waiting for his feet to fill them again. There was a small table under the window. Two unread books were placed on top of it, along with a broken watch and his money box. I couldn't take my eyes off that money box. I knew what it meant to Freddie and what it represented for him This was his future, his freedom . . . his escape route out of here.

His narrow cupboard was closed and, on the floor, nestled under the tatty wooden chair, was his football. I'd not touched it since he'd gone. I couldn't bring myself to.

Mine and Martha's side was a mess. Our shared bed with the tatty cover. Our clothes spilling on to the floor. Freddie used to moan about it so much. He said it made the room feel so much smaller when we were there, taking it over.

But right now, this small room had never felt so big.

'I got through the day,' I tell the vacant bed. 'I didn't blow myself up. But I have to get up early again tomorrow. I'm not feeling too bad about it. I survived my first day, at least. I hope I'll see that Grace again.' I smiled gently. 'I think you'd like her, Fred. She's dead funny.

And clever too. She's like the big sister I never had.'

Perhaps Grace could feel the missing space that Freddie had left, if only a little bit.

I wondered what Freddie would make of that – me working at the same place he had been for so long. I knew he wouldn't sneer, like Dad. He wouldn't say it was no place for girls – Freddie was never like that.

But I knew he would be worried for me. He always was.

I stared down at my own feet. Laced boots, bashed and already fraying at the toes. There was never any money for fancy things like new clothes and shoes. Even though I knew most of the women in the factory were in the same boat as me, I wondered how they still managed to look so good and be so confident, despite their woes. How do you get to be like that? Did you learn it, or was it something you were born with? Why couldn't I be a little more like that?

I'd like to think that if he were here, Freddie would reach out and touch my hand. He'd tell me to 'stop being a daft little beggar' and that I was fine as I was. Freddie would assure me that 'things will turn out for the best in the end'.

Because they always did, in Freddie's eyes. He always saw the good in everything.

I can't help thinking about him. I try not to, because it just makes the hurting inside worse. I can see what the worry does to Mam. She always said that Freddie wasn't built for fighting. Freddie had other plans for his life. I think of his money box and the coins he had squirrelled away inside. Freddie knew what he wanted to be – and a solider wasn't it.

All of this was so very wrong. The world seemed to be upside down and unfamiliar now, and it made the uneasy feelings in my stomach slip and slide about even more than usual.

I tried to picture him out there, oversees – knee deep in mud, perhaps, marching forward. Was he scared? Was he coping? Did he still think of us at all?

As I bit my lip, a question that I was trying so desperately to push away flooded my mind.

Would he even make it home at all?

Mam was sat in the front room when I went downstairs; this room also doubled up as her and Dad's bedroom. Her hands were folded in her lap and her face had that far-away look that meant she was thinking troubled thoughts again. Martha was drawing at the table. She lifted her head up when I walked into the room and beamed.

'Hettie is back,' she said loudly, in case no one else had realised.

Mam smiled wearily in my direction. I wasn't sure if she'd heard me creep in earlier. In truth, I had just wanted some quiet in my bedroom before I faced questions from the family.

'So, how did it go?' she asked.

I nodded, feeling shy. 'It was fine, I think. It was very busy and loud.' I touched my ears; I could still hear the ringing noises inside my head. Would it ever go away?

Mam sighed. 'I expect you'll soon get used to that . . .'

'Where's Dad?' I asked gently. It wasn't like I particularly expected him to be here waiting for me, asking me how my first day had gone . . . If he wasn't in the house, or at work, there was only one other place he would be.

'Where do you think he is?' Mam shot at me. Her eyes were blazing. 'Where does he always go when he can't face up to things?'

Face up to things? I flinched and looked towards Martha. Her head had dropped back down and she was continuing with her drawing, but I could see that her strokes were getting more frantic.

'What's wrong?' I dared to ask Mam.

She just shook her head dismissively. 'Nowt. Nowt is wrong.'

'He's at the pub then.' It wasn't a question.

'Aye.' Mam nodded sadly. 'I'm surprised he doesn't drink that place dry, he spends so much time in there.'

I turned away. Was it so bad that a tiny piece of me was relieved? At least today I wouldn't have to listen to any more of Dad's negative words. With any luck he'd drink himself silly on cheap ale and fall unconscious before he even reached his own bed.

I felt like a bad person thinking these thoughts.

'Mam is upset,' Martha said suddenly, still drawing. Her strokes were moving upwards, almost tearing through the paper. 'She's upset about Freddie and she told Dad so. She told Dad he was a "useless good for nothing" for letting Freddie go, because he was far too young. She said, "you should have . . . bloody well . . . stopped him".' Martha stumbled over the last few words, but then looked up proudly, as if seeking praise for getting the recollection right. 'I don't think Dad liked that much. He stormed out and slammed the door so hard the entire house shook almost off its hinges.'

I turned to Mam. She wasn't looking at me now. Her gaze was fixed on her clasped hands. Her very tightly clasped hands – so tight, in fact, that the tips of her fingers were white.

'Mam,' I said, the words suddenly dry in my throat.

'Has something happened to our Freddie?'

'No . . .' Her voice was drifting. 'Nothing has happened, love. Nothing at all.'

I wasn't stupid. I knew it had been months since we'd heard from Freddie. Mam waited at the letter box every morning with a mixture of hope and dread. Would the postman bring word from her son? Or would it be the day that we got that fateful telegram. The one that no one wanted to receive. The one that would tell us that our particular battle was over.

'Mam.' I stepped forward, touching her shoulder. 'What is it? What's wrong?'

'I had a dream.' Under my grip, I could feel her body trembling. 'You know about my dreams, Hettie. You know what they can mean. So many have come true.'

I said nothing. Inside I was frozen.

'In my dream, he was falling,' she whispered. 'He was falling, and I wasn't there to catch him . . .'

'That doesn't mean anything, Mam,' I said, even though I knew that wouldn't help to reassure her.

'He was falling . . .' she repeated thinly. 'My boy. He was gone and there was nothing I could do to help him. My whole family – torn apart – and there was nothing I could do.'

***

The next morning was cool and bright and the light drizzle helped to wake me as I left the house. This time, my stomach wasn't quite as full of knots and although I felt a shiver of apprehension as I turned my street corner, I realised that there was a bubble of excitement inside of me too. I was looking forward to seeing the girls again – to seeing Grace, Alice and Flo.

At the top of the road I saw Flo and Alice again. Flo was leant up against the red brick wall, her thick dark hair piled on top of her head in a curly mess. I decided she looked even more beautiful today. Like an exotic bird out of place in these bleak woods. Flo smiled as I approached and nudged Alice, who was stood next to her. Alice's hair was pinned tightly to her head in neat little waves.

'There you go, I said she'd come back,' Flo said brightly.

'Did you not think I would?' I said, a little put out.

Alice giggled. 'Well – you are just a slip of a thing, we did wonder if you'd survive.'

I frowned a little, wondering if Alice still thought of me as a child. I was just about to reply when Flo interrupted.

'Take no notice, Hettie. She's only teasing you. We knew you'd come back, that's why we waited for you. We wanted to walk in with you again – make sure you were all right.'

'And Grace would have our guts for garters if we didn't

look out for you,' Alice added. 'She's keen to make sure you're looked after.'

'Oh . . .' I said, a little surprised but also secretly chuffed. 'Well, thank you . . .'

'Proper little thing, aren't you,' Alice said, still smiling as we set off in the direction of the factory. 'All good manners and nice words. You must have been brought up well.'

'Unlike you!' Flo sniggered, nudging her friend. 'Last I heard, you were brought up with the alley cats in the yard.'

Alice nudged her back. 'Hey! You're hardly 'Miss La-di-da, neither!'

Both of them rolled up in laughter at this.

I thought of Mam, sat at home. How she had spent years making sure all of us could read our letters properly, that we knew our Ps and Qs, and how to present ourselves properly in the company of others. *We might not be from money,* she always said. *But that doesn't stop us trying to do better. It's no excuse for not being polite.*

I'm not sure Dad agreed with her. But then again, Dad didn't say much about that sort of thing anyway. I don't think it was one of his priorities.

'I'm only messing,' Flo said good-naturedly. 'Alice lives on Marsh Lane, Hettie – just round the corner from you. Her old man works on the railway as a clerk. She gets her cheeky charm from being part of a big family.'

I smiled, but didn't say anything. I wondered whether Alice's dad might know mine; Dad having worked on the railways. I hoped not. Dad wasn't one for making friends. If people knew of him, it wasn't usually for good reasons.

'Hey – you look a little pale, Hettie. Are you all right?' Flo asked. 'Did you find yesterday a bit hard?'

'It was fine,' I said. 'I think I'm a bit tired, that's all . . . and worried . . .' Both women stared at me curiously so I continued on, stumbling a little over my words. It was so hard to talk about my worries.

'It's my brother, Freddie – he was called up a few months ago. We've not heard from him in a while. Apart from one short letter, that's been it really.'

My words tumbled out before I remembered about Alice and her own brother. She was looking at her feet. Guilt washed over me. Why did I open my big gob?

'Ah!' said Flo. She didn't really have to say anything else. Everyone around here had someone they were worried about, whether it was a brother, father, uncle or sweetheart. I shouldn't have gone and made a big fuss about it and I felt awful, like I had spoken out of turn.

'It's hard for them to get letters home. Don't read too much into it,' Alice said kindly, tapping my arm.

'We waited for such a long time to hear from Tom and even though it wasn't good news in the end . . .' She shrugged sadly. 'You just have to keep hoping, don't you? It doesn't mean the same will happen to Freddie.'

We walked in silence for a bit. I noticed Alice was blinking a bit, as if fighting tears. I felt so bad for making her think about her brother again.

'It was so good that you met Grace properly yesterday,' Flo said suddenly. 'Grace already thinks a lot of you. She told us as much.'

'I really like her,' I replied, feeling proud. 'She was so brave, taking on the boys yesterday . . .'

'Aye, she has passion for football, that's for sure.' Flo paused. 'But you know – even Grace is struggling. She's waiting on word of her husband. It's been far too long now, and she's not heard a thing.'

Alice's face screwed up. 'It's not easy, is it? Poor Gracie.'

Flo peered over at me. 'How old is your Freddie, Hettie?'

'Just turned sixteen.' I paused, unsure whether to continue. 'It sounds silly, but my mam had a bad dream about him last night. She's worried sick now. Her dreams often come true, you see – well, they have before, so it's made her wonder . . .'

Flo breathed out hard. 'Oh, you don't believe in that

nonsense, do you? Next you'll be telling me you avoid black cats.'

I frowned and didn't dare mention that, yes, I would dart out of the way of a black cat *and* I'd never walk under a ladder!

Alice squeezed my arm gently. 'You shouldn't worry about things like that, Hettie. They're not real. You have enough to worry about in the here and now.'

I nodded. 'I know, but–'

Flo snorted. 'Dreams are just dreams, after all. Hey, if I paid attention to mine, it would mean I am likely to have tea with King George on the roof of the Ritz, and I can't see that happening any time soon.'

Both women burst out laughing and I found myself smiling despite myself.

'Now, let's have no more talk of daft dreams and predictions,' said Flo.

My cheeks reddened. 'Of course, Flo,' I said quietly.

But I couldn't help feeling a bit wobbly as we walked in the factory. Did I really fit in here, with these strong, confident women? Or was I just a silly little girl who had no place doing men's work.

The morning seemed longer than it did yesterday. My arms and back were aching by the time lunchtime came, and my eyes were smarting from concentrating on the task at hand. I was amazed by how the other women seemed able to work so quickly and effortlessly. I wondered if I would ever be the same. Despite not being allowed to talk, the women all did, murmuring quietly between themselves. Sometimes one or two of them would break into song. But I couldn't join in. All my attention had to be on the job in hand – packing the explosives carefully and handling the detonator. I was still terrified of making a mistake. One slip-up and I could go up in smoke! It was no wonder my fingers continued to shake.

By the time we'd filed into the canteen, my body was flagging. I was too tired to think about eating and as I collected my food, I couldn't even imagine eating it. My mouth felt too dry and all I longed to do was to sit down and close my eyes for a few minutes.

'Are you all right, lass?'

I turned to find Grace standing behind me, a warm smile spread across her face, and immediately my mood brightened. Alice was stood next to her, also grinning. She gave me a wink in welcome.

'I'm all done in,' I admitted. 'Is it time to go home yet?'

Grace laughed. 'Sadly not, love, but you can at least rest your feet while you listen to the funny story I've got for you.'

'You're going to love this,' Alice said, nudging me.

Intrigued, I followed Grace and Alice to a large table at the back of the room. I noticed that a few of the lads, including George, Harry and Billy, were sitting at the far end. They looked up as we approached, then quickly flicked their gaze away again. They seemed deeply involved in their conversation. Harry had a scowl etched across his face. Other women I recognised were sitting at the table, including Flo. There was also a short, stocky woman sitting opposite. She had short brown hair and a pretty, friendly face that seemed immediately open to conversation.

Grace nudged the woman gently. 'Budge up, Gertie. There's room for three more here.'

The woman, Gertie, looked up and sighed loudly. At first I thought she was protesting, but then I saw a smile curl her lips. 'You are a right bossy one, Grace Sibbert,' she said.

'You know me too well,' Grace replied. 'But thought you might also be interested in some news I heard this morning.'

Flo sat up straighter. 'Tell us more, Gracie, tell us more. You know I like a good story.'

I would have imagined that Grace would lower her voice to tell us this interesting tale, but instead she sat back on her chair, her focus fixed on the lads across from us. Her voice became as loud and bright as a clergyman's.

'I heard that our boys suffered a loss at their football game last night. In fact . . .' She paused, her gaze still fixed on their faces. 'It wasn't so much a loss, as downright slaughter.'

Flo exploded with laughter. 'Oh, do tell me more!'

'Apparently, poor old George stormed off in tears,' Alice added loudly. 'I don't think our boy likes losing, much.'

'Funny that – you'd think he'd be used to it,' Grace said sweetly. 'He still needs to go and fetch us that chocolate he owes us.'

Across the table, George shifted forwards. His cheeks were bright red and his eyes gleaming with what looked like rage. 'Pay no mind to them, lads,' he said loudly to those around him. 'What do these women know anyway? The only thing they are good for is cooking and gossiping.'

'Is that right, George Roberts?' Grace's voice was like sheet ice, but her eyes were still lit up with mirth. 'We know nowt, eh?'

'Nowt about football, that's for sure,' George shot back. 'What gives you the right to mouth off, anyway? You score a couple of lucky shots against us yesterday and now you think you know it all?'

'I tell you what, George – I'm probably a damn sight better than the lot of you,' Grace replied calmly. 'You're only lucky we didn't have Gertie with us yesterday. Or Florrie Rance here – she has an even better shot than me.'

I looked up. A tall, pretty woman sitting next to Gertie was grinning widely. I took it that she was the Florrie Rance in question.

'Yeah, right,' George scoffed. 'It was luck that helped you yesterday, nowt else.'

Alice snorted at this. 'Florrie's not the only one, either. I've seen your lads run. Most of them look as if they've got their legs tied together.'

George's face was pulled into a sneer. He shook his head slowly. 'What? You kick a ball through a window and now you think you can play for Preston North End?'

Grace shrugged. 'Reckon I could give it a go. Reckon a lot of us girls could.'

Flo called over, 'You know I'd be up for it. I'm faster than most of those lads and they know it. I can't play straight away because I need to get some boots. But once I do, I'll be game.'

Grace grinned back at her. 'Sure you will, Flo Redford. And there are others. Alice Kell here, obviously – who's friends with Gertie Whittle over there. You know Gertie, don't you?' Gertie waved delicately in the boys' direction as Grace turned her focus fully on us. 'Then there's Evelyn Clayton too. I've seen her move the ball well. Florrie Rance here, who I've mentioned.'

'I'll be happy to give it go,' Florrie Rance said brightly.

'And there's the other Alice,' Grace continued, counting on her fingers. 'Alice Standing. I've talked to her before about playing – I know she'd be keen.'

'There's plenty,' Flo said smoothly. 'And a few more that we can teach how to play. With a bit of practice they could be strong or fast on the ball.'

'It'll be good for us,' Grace murmured, like she was thinking out loud. 'The bosses should want to support us improving our bodies and minds and all that . . .'

'I think they meant needlework,' Alice replied dryly.

'I'm not sure they'd approve of us girls playing a man's sport.'

Grace snorted. 'I don't give a stuff. We can start getting some names together. See who's interested. It'll be good to know numbers.'

A glow of excitement surged through me. I couldn't believe what Grace was suggesting. It was so brave of her to think these things, let alone say them.

'Well, I'm definitely in,' Flo announced.

'And me,' said Gertie.

'Me three,' added Florrie Rance.

Grace turned to me. 'How about you, Hettie? I bet you'd be fast on the pitch. Have you ever played properly before?'

I hesitated, feeling shy again. 'Well . . . yes. A bit. I mean, I used to play with my brother.'

'Would you like to have a go with us?' she asked gently.

My cheeks reddened. 'I–I dunno. I haven't played an actual game before . . .'

'Neither have many of us,' Flo said. 'But that's part of the fun of it. We can learn together.'

'My dad won't like it,' I muttered. 'He doesn't approve of things like this.'

Grace placed her hand on my arm. 'Remember what we spoke of before, Hettie. About there being a need to change. You agreed with that, didn't you? Don't you want to be part of it all?'

I thought of Freddie's words. How he would look off into the distance, as if he could see a brighter future right there in front of him, as if he could actually touch it. *Things will get better, Hettie. I know it. We can make it happen.*

Something within me stirred. My, how I missed Freddie. How I wished he was here with me now. But I also knew what he'd want me to do.

'All right, I'll give it a go,' I said.

Grace winked at me and then sat back in her seat and folded her arms, a smug expression spread across her face. 'Well, George – it seems to me that we could have the beginnings of a decent football team here.'

George scoffed. 'So?' Then his eyes widened and he barked out an abrupt cough. 'My God, Grace, surely you're not suggesting that you could take my boys on? I mean, sure, create a nice little team for yourselves, but don't go thinking you can beat the likes of us.'

'That's exactly what I'm suggesting.' Her voice was light, yet cool. 'And I don't *think* we can beat you. I *know* we can.'

He laughed. 'Big words, Grace Sibbert. Seriously – you're off your rocker.'

'Oh, we'll see, won't we?' Grace replied smoothly. 'We'll

see who's laughing when my girls have played your boys.'

'Played my *men*,' George emphasised curtly.

'Oh... is that what they are?' Grace flashed him a perfect smile. 'Because I've heard something quite different.'

Out in the yard a little later, I stood with Grace and Flo and a few others as they watched the lads kick the tatty football along the ground. Alice had taken herself off, complaining of a headache, but Flo confided to us that Alice was feeling sad about her brother. I wondered if all this talk of football was bringing her feelings back.

I felt bad for Alice as I stood with the others. If anyone knew what it was like to miss a brother, it was me. God knows what I would be like if anything were to happen to Freddie – it really didn't bear thinking about. At least here, I could distract myself watching the lads play. They really were a motley lot and not the most skilled. At one point, George took the ball and almost tripped over it in his efforts to get away from another player. We giggled as we watched and George turned to face us, his face flushed with rage.

'You wait!' he shouted, his back stiff and his head held high. 'We'll soon show you!'

'Are we barmy?' Grace asked suddenly, when George had

returned to the game. 'I mean, are we . . . really? Thinking we can take them on?'

'It's just kicking a football around, Grace,' one of the other women said stoutly. She was busy sucking on her cigarette and, judging by the cough that followed her words, I didn't reckon on her ability to be able to run far on the pitch.

'It's not though, Aggie,' Grace scolded. Her face was now pinched white and she drew her arms across her chest in a defensive fashion. 'It's not as easy as you think. My husband used to play . . .' Her voice broke a little but she shook it off quickly. 'And when I were a lass, I used to play with some of the younger lads. There's tactics to consider and you need to be fast and strong. Stronger than them, anyway . . .'

'We can be, though,' Flo said smoothly. 'You know how fast I am, and plenty of these women have played before with their brothers or mates. We're not so different from the boys.'

'I know,' Grace said stiffly. 'And I want to prove as much.'

Aggie shuffled forward. 'You could put Evelyn Clayton in goal. She used to do it as a kid, before they told her off for being a girl and asked her to leave.' She giggled. 'Her hair used to be so short I reckon they never noticed.'

Grace's face lit up. 'There's an idea . . . Florrie, could you persuade that Peggy girl who works next to you? I've heard she's fast.'

Florrie shrugged. 'I don't see why not.'

Aggie sniffed. 'I wish I could do more, but you know – my lungs aren't up to much.' She wrinkled her nose. 'I could cut up oranges for you for half-time.'

'That would be great,' Grace replied. 'I'll have a word with Alice Standing too. I've chatted to her before about the game. I really think she might be keen. And it's good that Gertie and Florrie want to be involved.'

'Florrie is meant to be a great striker,' Flo said, smiling. 'But of course she would be, with a name like that. Us Florences always are wonderful!'

'What about Alice?' Grace probed. 'Do you think she'll consider it?'

Flo lowered her head a little. 'I'm not sure – I'm really not. I know she'd love to, in many ways. But she's still so upset about her Tom . . .'

'I understand. Perhaps she could just come and watch? Cheer us on, like?'

Flo nodded. 'I'll ask her.'

'Thank you.' Grace turned to me. 'Our Hettie here is going to join in too, aren't you, pet?'

I glanced up, seeing everyone's eyes on me. Despite the nerves that prickled my skin, I felt a buzz of excitement bubbling along my spine.

'Yes,' I said, nodding. 'Well, I'm going to give it a go, any road.'

Grace nodded back. 'Great, that's as good a start as any. I will talk to the other girls, then. See who's interested – even if they just want to come and watch at first, it might help. This is it, girls. This is the start of it, you know.'

'The start of what?' asked Aggie, looking confused.

Grace burst out laughing and thumped her gently on the arm.

'The start of something wonderful. Just you wait, Aggie.' Her eyes were gleaming with joy. 'Us Dick, Kerr Girls are going to show the boys what we are made of. We are going to win.'

With that amount of enthusiasm – it was impossible not to believe her.

Walking home, I felt a strange surge of energy ripple inside of me.

We were going to play a game, a *real* game of football against the lads at Dick, Kerr and not one of the girls appeared to be remotely nervous about it. I was, of course, but I kept that hidden. I didn't want the others to think I was babyish or weak. But I was excited too.

'I reckon I have eleven confirmed girls,' Grace had said as we walked out of the factory. 'Eleven girls keen as mustard to wipe the smiles off those boys' faces.'

'Do you really think we can do it?' I asked, still feeling unsure. After all, these boys played together all the time. They were loud and confident. They were certain they would give us a good pasting.

Grace simply patted my arm. 'Let's just see, Hettie. We might surprise them.' She puffed out her chest proudly and cast her eyes back towards the direction of the factory. 'And even if don't, we'll have good fun trying. We have nothing to lose, really.'

Good fun. I didn't say it then, because I didn't want to sound daft, but I could barely remember the last time I'd had fun. In recent times the war had weighed heavy over us and Dad's increasingly bad temper was a constant drain on all the family. We'd never said it openly, though – it was easier, I suppose, not to talk about our worries. Not to think about them.

I stepped through the front door, still feeling that ripple of excitement. I could hear the soft murmurings of Mam and Martha talking in the kitchen. I followed the sound of their voices and found them sitting at the table. Mam was combing out Martha's long, wild hair. On the table in front of the them was some needlework that they must have been working on together, and behind, on the stove, bubbled a grey-looking stew. I knew it was probably tripe again, and my stomach curdled at the thought, but I didn't say anything. I didn't want to anger Mam. I knew she would've done her best with what little ingredients she could afford this week.

'Good day?' Mam asked without looking up. 'You're a bit late.'

'I was talking to some of the girls after,' I said and then added cautiously, 'they've asked me to play a game with them this Saturday.'

Mam looked up, her eyes were sharp. The comb was

gripped in her hand like some kind of deadly weapon. 'Game? What sort of game?'

'Football. We are to play the boys from the factory.' I paused and then quickly added, 'The boys aren't very good.'

This obviously made no difference to Mam, who was looking at me in disappointment. 'Hettie – you are there to work. Not to mess around with boys.' She chewed on her lip. 'My God, what would your father say?'

I said nothing, instead I simply stared back at her. We both knew what my dad would say. His closed, angry face would darken even further. His eyes would squint in my direction, as if looking at my face was too painful, too shocking. It would be yet another reason for Dad to be disappointed in me.

'It's just a game, Mam,' I said quietly. 'We were messing round a bit at lunch, and some of the girls challenged the boys. The boys keep losing their matches so it's not going to be hard. We think we might actually beat them. Fancy that?'

'But what will people think?' Her voice was sharp, biting through the air between us. 'What will they think about a young girl running around with her legs on show? Getting muddy? Shouting and screaming like you're as common as muck.'

'It's one game,' I said carefully. 'I won't shout and scream and I promise to do my chores after.' I moved closer to her and gently touched her hand. 'Please, Mam . . .'

'Oh, let her, Mam,' Martha said suddenly, her bright voice breaking the tension. 'Hettie really wants to, can't you tell? Won't you let her?'

Martha was staring up at Mam. She was the only one in the family able to win both Mam and Dad's affections equally. It was frustrating sometimes, but today I was thankful for it.

Mam sighed; the sound came from deep within her and seemed to make her entire body shudder. 'OK, Hettie,' she said finally. 'But just this one game, mind. Just one game. Then afterwards you can help me scrub the lav.'

I cringed. That was the very worst job she could give me, of course. I fixed a smile on my face and tried not to think too much about the dirty task that would await me.

'Thank you, Mam,' I said sincerely.

'One thing, though . . .' Her pale face turned away from me again and back towards her needlework. 'You're not to mention a word of this to your father – do you hear? Not a word. That goes for you too, Martha.'

We both nodded solemnly.

'Because if he gets wind of this,' she muttered, her fingers flailing at the cloth. 'You know what'll happen.'

Mam once told me that she was born into money. Not huge riches, like those mansion houses outside of town, but certainly into more money than we have now. Her father, my grandfather, was a master builder. They lived in a house twice the size of our one, and they didn't even have to share the lavvy! Mam was always most proud of the fact that her dad owned his own horse and cart – that was a sign of wealth in those days.

She was only young when he died, a year or so older than Martha is now. The story goes that he was talking to a man about a job, and was so deep in conversation that he stepped out in the road in front of a bike. My grandfather was apparently a very skinny, frail man and was knocked over easily, banging his head on the hard cobbles.

Things changed for Mam then. She ended up moving just a few streets away from here – her, Nan and her two little sisters were now suddenly sharing a dank and dark basement room. I think Mam's view on everything changed then. She knew that life could be cruel and hard and that you could easily have something good taken away from you, even if you didn't deserve it.

'You have to make do with what life serves you,' she would say to me and Martha. 'Never expect too much and then you can't be disappointed.'

We'd both nod back at her, our faces all serious. We'd never dare to raise objections to Mam's views, but even so, there was many a time when I found myself biting my tongue and fighting the words that longed to escape.

But what if there is better, Mam? What if we can make our lives better for ourselves?

I may have never said those words out loud, but they still settled in my head. I still listened to them.

I still hoped that life could be better than this. It really could.

It wasn't a question of whether or not we deserved it – it was a question of believing it.

'Do you really like it . . . football?'

Martha was pressed up next to me in bed. Her cold little legs were like ice cubes against me. Often I wished the bed was bigger, so that I could pull away and gain some space of my own, but tonight I just drew the scratchy blanket tighter over us, so that it was digging into our necks.

'I do,' I said. 'At least, I think I do. I've never really played before, not an actual game, like.'

Martha worried at her face. It was scrubbed fresh and pink from her bath. 'Then how do you know you'll be any good at it? You might be rubbish.'

'I might . . . that's true . . .'

My voice drifted. Thoughts began to niggle at me again. What good could I be? I was just some silly girl who used to muck around with her brother in the yard. I'd only seen a handful of games myself, and all of those had been Freddie and his mates over at the rec.

My heart skipped. I didn't even know all the rules! Offside? Fouls? Blimey, I would be made to look like such a fool.

'You should just run fast,' Martha said matter-of-factly. 'And kick anyone that comes near you.'

I giggled. 'I think I might get into trouble for doing that.'

'But at least it'll look like you're trying.'

'I suppose . . .'

'Are the other girls good?'

I rolled over so that I was facing Martha. Her face was pressed up against the mattress and her blonde hair was spread behind in a golden fan. She was gazing at me with an intensity, it was almost as if she could see right inside of me.

'I think a lot of them are really good,' I said. 'Grace, Flo and Alice are meant to be amazing. Apparently Florrie Rance is an excellent striker and a girl called Evelyn is a great keeper. They are so confident too, like they aren't frightened of anything.'

'They're not frightened of silly boys,' Martha's nose curled up and a tiny smile sparked on her face. 'I'm not either. Ronnie from two doors down thinks he can beat me at everything. But he can't. I'm faster than him. And tougher. Yesterday, I punched him on the nose for calling me a sissy and he's the one who went home crying.'

'You punched Ronnie?' I hissed. I thought of his mam, who was a stern sort and not someone you'd be likely to mess with. 'Does Mam know?'

Martha flinched a little. 'No . . . I thought she'd be angry with at me.'

'You think . . . ?' I snorted. 'Don't worry, Martha. If she's not heard about it yet, she's not likely to. But you shouldn't be going around punching people. There's other ways to show that you're strong and tough.'

'Like playing football?'

'I suppose,' I whispered, although I certainly didn't feel that way. If only I could steal just a tiny bit of Martha's spirit.

'What will you wear?' Martha asked suddenly.

I rolled on to my back and sighed. I hadn't even thought about that. I certainly didn't own a football kit and I was pretty sure I couldn't turn up on Saturday wearing my Sunday-best dress.

'You could wear Freddie's stuff . . .' Martha said softly. 'He wouldn't mind.'

'Eh?'

'You could wear his shorts and his boots. It's all in his cupboard. I look at it sometimes.'

I paused, not sure what to say. I didn't know that Martha still looked at his things too. I reached across and took her small, cool hand in mine and squeezed it.

'That's not such a bad idea,' I said.

'Really?'

'Really. Freddie isn't much bigger than me, so his shorts, and even a top, should fit me fine. His boots might be too big, but if I wear a couple of pairs of socks . . .'

'It'll work,' Martha mumbled. 'I know it will.'

I snuggled down next to her, suddenly pleased for her body next to mine. 'It really might,' I admitted.

'You must do it,' she said softly. 'You really must play. Because if you don't, you'll always wonder, won't you . . .'

'Wonder what?'

'Wonder if you were good enough.' She yawned. 'Mam always tells us to try our best at everything we do. So you should try your best at this. You can do it, Hettie. I'm sure of it.'

I pulled her towards me. 'Then if you're sure of it, so am I.'

'Hettie . . .' Martha's voice was barely a whisper now; she was drifting off to sleep.

'What, my dear?'

'Can I play football like you one day? Like Freddie did, too . . . I want to play.'

I leant over and kissed the top of her head.

'One day, Martha,' I whispered. 'I think so, one day.'

My focus switched to the other side of the room, where Freddie's bed was lit up by the moon's rays feeding through the window. In this pale light, his football seemed to be glowing.

'Goodnight, Fred,' I whispered into the air. 'Keep safe.'

Keep safe for me, for all of us.

I closed my eyes and dreamt once more that I was playing football with him. That we were laughing and joking around.

I dreamt that we were happy again.

By the time the weekend came, I was near exhausted from the job. As soon as I woke on Saturday morning, I had to wait a moment before easing myself out of bed. I was beginning to think that every one of my muscles had been worked half to death, and that included muscles I didn't even know were there before.

In the kitchen, Mam was cooking some porridge on the stove. I was grateful for the heat from the pot on such a bitter morning. I stood beside her and warmed my hands.

'Now, don't you go putting your fingers in,' she scolded. 'And, if you do that for too long, you'll end up with chilblains.'

Dad was already dressed for work. I watched as he supped down the last of his tea and then checked his face in the mirror. His hair was freshly combed and his face was soft and clean-shaven. He always liked to look neat. Only the dark shadows under his eyes gave away the mood that I knew lurked deep inside of him. I wondered how much his back was hurting today. He would never openly complain, but I could tell by the way that he moved and how he cried out in the night that the pain was bad.

It wasn't fair that he still had to go out and work on the docks, but what choice did he have? We needed the money more than ever now, what with Freddie's wages stopping. Of course, mine were half what my brother earnt.

'Are you excited about the match today, Hettie?' Martha asked brightly.

I think she spoke before thinking. She often did that – blurting out thoughts without paying mind to who was in the room. I saw her little cheeks turn pink as she realised her mistake.

'Eh? Match?' Dad turned towards me. 'What match?'

I scowled at Martha. I couldn't help myself. She looked like she was about to cry. I immediately felt bad.

'It's nowt, really,' I said, trying to sound flippant. 'Not really a match at all – just a kick-about with some of the girls from work.'

Dad raised one eyebrow. 'And you think that's a good way to spend your time? I've told you before about messing about with football – it's not right for young girls. You should be helping your mother around the house. Don't you think she needs the help?'

Guilt prickled me. I knew she needed help. I didn't

want him to think I wasn't going to do my bit. 'Dad—'

'She can help me after,' Mam said bluntly. 'I'm sure a few hours in the fresh air will do her the world of good, Stan. Look at her face, it's as pale as milk. She needs the exercise.'

'She'll get enough exercise if she works hard enough,' Dad replied. 'I can't approve of my girl playing football with other women. It's just not right.'

Mam's face was calm. She stirred the porridge slowly. 'Perhaps not, but it's not as if it's a proper game, Stan. It'll just be some women running around on the rec. No one will pay any notice to them.'

I realised that she hadn't mentioned that we were going to be playing against the lads. I looked towards her, but she simply shook her head quickly at me. I couldn't help smiling. Mam was protecting me. She didn't want me to get into any trouble.

Did that mean she approved?

Dad grunted. 'I just don't like the idea of my girl running around with other women. What will that look like?'

'Like someone having fun?' Mam said quietly. 'God knows we could do with more of that around here.'

The silence was like an icy cloak. I saw Dad's back stiffen. He dragged his eyes away from me, then, sniffing, he picked up his jacket from the chair and pulled it on.

'I see,' he said finally. 'It's like that, is it?'

'It's not "like" anything . . .' Mam said, continuing to stir the porridge. 'It's just a fact. That's all.'

'Well. It looks like the decision has already been made.' He stamped out of the room, not bothering to look back. 'Don't you blame me when the neighbours start gossiping about our wayward child. I'm telling you now – this is a one-off, right? A one off!'

Our rickety front door slammed and Mam flinched.

'It's all right, Mam,' I said. 'I won't go. I'll stay here with you.'

She turned and shook her spoon at me. Tiny droplets of porridge fell to the floor, but she didn't seem to notice or care.

'Oh, you'll go,' she said sharply. 'After that performance by your father, you have to. It's an order.'

'All right . . .' I said, feeling uneasy.

'And you'll have fun,' she added quickly. 'That's an order too.'

I half ran to the park, wearing one of Mam's battered old coats to protect me from the icy-cold wind that seemed to be blasting through the streets at full pelt. I'd found a pair of Freddie's old football socks bundled up in his drawer and had pulled them on, aware of how daft they looked pulled up high over my reedy white legs. His boots were far too big on me, but another pair of socks helped keep them a little more secure. I was silently praying that they wouldn't suddenly fly off. His shorts were also far too big, but I folded over the waistband and hitched them up as high as I could get away with – also praying that they wouldn't slide down. There were so many things that could go wrong today and each one of them was making me feel a little more queasy.

'You look grand,' Mam had said, before I'd left. This had been the most complimentary thing she'd said to me in ages, so I had set off from the house feeling quite cheery.

That feeling soon began to slip away as I edged towards the field. I could see a small group of men warming up by the side of the pitch. They were laughing loudly and shouting among themselves. I couldn't see the other girls anywhere. Suddenly I was aware of my thin, worn shirt and far-too-big-for-me shorts. I was like a little girl playing dress-up in her brother's clothes.

'Hey!' one of the lads called out. 'Here's one of them, look!'

I clutched my coat closer to me and smiled feebly. In fairness, the boy who had shouted seemed friendly enough, but even so, he had made my insides do somersaults.

'She's blimmin' tiny. We could knock her over by blowing on her,' another shouted. I glanced over and saw that it was George. He was looking at me with a face like thunder.

I felt very exposed and nervous. Where were the other girls?

'Ey up!'

I spun round and to my relief saw that Grace was heading my way. A small group trailed behind her, chattering brightly and squinting against the mid-morning sun.

For a moment, I just stood there watching them, gawping like an idiot. I couldn't quite believe how good the girls looked. Grace's hair was swept away from her face, which was glowing with excitement. Another girl had pinned her hair back and her grin was stretched from cheek to cheek. All of them were dressed in dark shorts and different coloured long-sleeve jerseys. Some even had neat little caps pinned on their heads.

'Hettie, you came!' Grace rushed towards me, still beaming. 'Isn't this marvellous? The rain has stayed away. It really is glorious weather.'

'And you've got a team!' I said.

Grace beamed. 'Exactly. Eleven girls, ready to play!' She pointed at the three standing directly behind her, who waved in my direction. 'Alice Standing, Florrie Rance and Evelyn Clayton – this is Hettie.'

I waved back shyly. They all looked so tall and strong. Yet again, I was desperately aware of my own tiny, bony stance.

More women were tramping up the field to meet us. It has to be said – some looked more pleased about it than others. I spotted Gertie and waved at her and she winked back. Even better, Alice Kell and Flo were there. They were standing just aside from the group and not dressed in their kit – but they had come! I walked over to them.

'We thought we'd come and watch for a bit,' Flo said brightly. 'We can't play today, but I will do next time. I'm already planning to buy my boots next week and Alice is coming around to the idea."

Alice nodded in agreement. 'Yeah, Flo persuaded me to come along. I can't quite believe Grace got a team together.' She half smiled. 'I can't help but be interested.'

'You should play,' I said to her. 'It might – well, it might help.'

Alice scanned my face as if searching for the right response. 'You know, Grace said the same thing.'

She paused. 'Aye, you might be right. I do miss playing so much and I know Tom would want me to keep it up.'

Flo rubbed her back. 'He would indeed. You know that.'

'So . . . maybe you'll think about playing next time, then?' I asked, hardly believing this was me being pushy and confident.

She smiled shyly. 'Aye – I might. I promise I'll think about it. But you need to stop fretting about me. The girls are waiting for you.'

'Good luck!' said Flo, punching my arm gently. 'Give those daft lads what for.'

'I'll do my best,' I promised.

I strolled back over to the main group of girls. Grace was deep in conversation with them, talking to each girl in turn and reassuring those who had nerves.

'We'll be fine,' Grace said firmly. 'Some of us are more experienced than others – but if we all pull together, we will be fine.'

We nodded in agreement. She was right. We could do this.

Grace walked us to the side of the pitch. I glanced over to where the boys were still warming up. They kept looking across at us and shouting out at us.

'Ignore them,' Florrie Rance said. 'They're just scared, that's all.'

Grace gathered us together in a huddle. 'We need to warm up too,' she said briskly. 'I know what to do, I've seen my husband do it enough when he used to play. We need to stretch our muscles, jog on the spot, get our blood pumping.'

'As long as it's just pumping in my body and nowhere else,' Gertie muttered. She was looking quite pale.

'The trick is to catch these boys when they're not expecting it,' Florrie Rance hissed at us. 'Yes, they are strong and quick, but we know they can be beaten. I've been speaking to young Harry over there and he's been giving me some inside information.'

Alice Standing giggled. 'Oh, has that poor boy still got his eye on you, Florrie?'

Florrie batted her eyelashes delicately. 'Well, pity for their team if he does. He certainly likes to open up to me.'

'Oh . . .' breathed Grace. 'Do tell us more.'

'Well . . .' Florrie's eyes widened, obviously enjoying this. 'Apparently, our sweet boys have some weaknesses. Old Frank there, in defence . . .' She pointed at a lanky kid with knobbly knees. 'He has no pace, so he can be outrun easily. Then there's Pete, on the wing. He always tackles from the left, so remember to turn him and take him on, on the right. Walt in goal is pretty useless too and barely moves from his spot – so if in doubt, take a shot.'

Grace puffed out her cheeks. 'I'm putting you up front, Florrie. I can't think of a better striker.'

'Sounds good to me,' Florrie agreed. 'I fancy getting myself a goal today.'

'Alice, you're going in central defence and Gertie you can go midfield. Play up high, just behind the striker. You're big and strong. If in doubt, shoot!' Gertie shrugged in agreement and Grace continued to give out positions, sounding ever more confident with each one.

'What about me?' I dared to ask quietly. 'Where are you playing me?'

Grace grinned, her attention now fully on me. 'You – my little whipper-snapper, are going on the wing. I want you to run, and I want you to knacker out these lads. Got it?'

I nodded, still a bit unsure but the bubble of excitement had returned.

'We can do this, girls,' Grace said firmly. 'I know we can. The Dick, Kerr Girls can win this.'

We all cheered in agreement.

The game started in a bit of a blur. Grace kicked off quickly and sent the ball soaring to the right wing, where another young player, Peggy, picked it up neatly.

I don't think the boys were prepared for us to attack so quickly and were practically frozen in shock. With quick feet, Peggy managed to turn one of the less-fit boys and side-foot a pass to me. Looking up, I spotted Florrie moving towards the eighteen-yard line. Realising that I had a defender coming in to tackle me, I had to make a quick decision: I released the ball quickly to Florrie and thankfully it landed perfectly in front of her. I thanked every saint I could think of under my breath. With the quickest feet I had ever seen, Florrie took the ball neatly with her right boot and then blasted it into the goal. It flew into the goal, top corner.

I yelled louder than I've ever done in my life, icy-cold air blasting my chest as I inhaled, but I didn't care. We all rushed to Florrie, who was suddenly swamped in excited girls.

We jumped up and down, giggling and laughing with glee.

'What a goal!'

'Florrie! You darling!'

'You had the keeper on his fat behind'

'Hettie! What an assist!'

The last comment was made by Grace, who winked in my direction. I felt myself blush with pride. Truth be told,

I was surprised that I had managed to make any impact at all. The rush of excitement flooding my body was almost overwhelming.

'C'mon girls, there's still a game to play here!' Gertie said, standing with her hands on her hips, looking quite put out. She hadn't yet touched the ball.

The first half continued, full of energy. The boys made some surging runs but were soon met in defence by Alice and Grace. We had them on their toes and they didn't like it. A few misfired shots were made towards our goal, but were so far off target, we found ourselves howling with laughter.

'C'mon lads! You can do better than that!' Gertie shouted.

'We're only girls, after all!' Grace reminded them. 'You should be beating us across the park.'

The boys looked red-faced and frustrated and for the rest of the half, we managed to keep a lot of the possession, moving the ball carefully between ourselves. Our mood was upbeat and confident. I even found I could make a few runs of my own. I remembered what Freddie had taught me, keeping the ball close to my feet and looking up to check for space. To my own surprise, I managed to control the ball with ease and loved the feeling of running at speed.

It was so freeing. I also loved to hear the other girls cheering me on.

'That's it, Hettie!'

'Look at her go!'

For once I didn't feel like the little new girl, full of nerves and worries. Instead I felt at least six feet tall and full of as much confidence and bravado as any man I had met – not that that was many!

It was a wonderful feeling.

Florrie had another shot on goal, but hit the post. Her arms flew up to her head in frustration. We could've taken a two-nil win.

I ran back to my position on the wing, wondering if it was going to stay this easy. Certainly some of the boys looked unfit and out of practice; it was a bit of a lopsided game.

That was all to change with the blow of the whistle for half-time. We continued the game immediately, not even pausing for breath. The lads, of course, were quite fired up by now and I could see a few of them were rattled by the early lead. They worked hard to keep possession and drove the ball hard into our half, testing our defence. It wasn't long before they equalised with a neat header and then put a powerful volley from outside the box just wide of the goal.

The boys continued to attack our half and it was clear that we were buckling a little under the pressure. Then Alice Standing, in panic, managed to deflect one shot in my direction. I managed to control the ball and bring it down to my feet, but, looking up, I realised that there was no one free to pass to. I had no other option but to drive forward.

I moved down the left wing, faintly aware of the lumbering force of the boys' main central defender coming towards me. All I knew was that I needed to release the ball into our box to create another chance.

I saw Gertie again, signalling for the ball. I didn't have long to make my decision. A defender was coming in tight on Gertie, if I played the ball to her there was a risk she would lose possession.

I looked beyond her, towards the goal. In the back of my mind I heard Freddie's voice.

Guide the ball to where it needs to be. Focus on the point and guide it in.

The point was the top-right corner. I took a breath and then, before I could second-guess myself, I lofted the ball upwards, hoping that I'd added just enough curl to place the ball where I needed it to be.

I closed my eyes. I couldn't look. I didn't dare.

If I'd missed, Gertie would be so cross. I could've

played it to her – instead, I took a massive risk.

The roar was overwhelming. All I could hear was the girls cheering and whooping with joy. I didn't move from my spot. I couldn't bring myself to. Instead, Grace ran over to me and wrapped me up in her arms.

'Hettie! What a shot! What a blinding shot. I can't believe you just did that.'

The truth was – neither could I!

The scenes were rather extraordinary once the full-time whistle blew. The result had remained at two-two. The lads seemed both disappointed and shocked by the result. Some were respectful in defeat, patting us on the back and commending us for a 'jolly good show'. Others were a little more bitter; George in particular. He took the match ball and kicked it to the other side of the pitch.

'It was luck, that's all.' He glowered at us before stalking off. 'We'll soon show you.'

Harry, on the hand, was very graceful in defeat. He ran off to retrieve the ball and returned it to Grace, handing it to her carefully like it was a precious stone.

'Usually the winners keep the ball,' he said, in a begrudging tone. 'And I suppose I have to admit that there was only one winner today.'

Grace was beaming; I don't think I've ever seen someone look so happy. She gripped the ball between her hands and held it aloft in front of the girls. The whole team was there, including Flo and Alice, who had managed to stay for the whole game.

'We did it!' she squealed. 'We beat the boys!'

The women all cheered back. Including me. In fact, I think I may have cheered the loudest. My lungs were full of air and, despite the amount of running I had done, I barely felt tired. In fact, my muscles were buzzing with energy.

'That was a wonderful effort,' Grace said. 'We were strong and brave, but more importantly – we were a team.'

We nodded, looking at one another with pride. Gertie even wiped a tear from her face.

Alice hugged me and Grace in turn. 'Honestly, you were amazing,' she said. 'It was so exciting to watch. Hettie – what a goal! I didn't think you had it in you.'

I grinned back. 'I'm glad I was able to surprise you.'

'Well, you certainly did! I was itching to join in,' Flo added. 'I'm going to have to get myself some proper boots now, aren't I?'

We all laughed in agreement.

Grace turned to me. Her hand took mine and squeezed it gently. 'Do you see now, Hettie, why I love this game so much? When you're out there playing, nothing else matters. All your worries, your problems – they slip to the back of your mind. All that matters is the team. All you care about is helping your team to win.'

I nodded quickly. 'I think I really do understand it, Grace. It was so wonderful to be part of it. It was exciting. It was . . .'

I struggled to find the right word. Grace squeezed my hand again.

'It was freedom,' she finished for me.

She was right. Of course she was. For the first time in for ever, I had felt free. For a short time I was allowed to simply be me. A football player. A part of a team.

'You need to believe,' Grace said, as the girls continued to chatter behind us. 'You need to believe that you can change your own life.'

'I'm starting to,' I whispered back.

Grace let go of my hand, but her smile remained. 'Good,' she said. 'Because I've got the feeling this is just the beginning.'

As soon as I walked through the front door, the excitement that had been bursting out of me began to trickle away. I was painfully aware of my scuffed knees and dirty top. I'd already taken my muddy boots off outside the house and these dangled in my hand like a lifeless trophy. I didn't dare look in the mirror, as I was sure my hair was a right fright. I must've looked like I had been dragged through a hedge backwards.

I paused in the dimly lit hallway, listening for voices. I could hear the sharp rise and fall of Mam talking with occasional interjections from Martha, who was laughing loudly. My spirits lifted. Martha would never dare to be so loud if Dad were at home. That must mean he was still working, or at the pub. Either way, he wasn't here to see the state of me.

I walked into the kitchen feeling strangely confident.

'Hettie!' Martha looked up from the mixing bowl she was stirring and then promptly burst out laughing.

Mam turned to me, hands on her hips. A slight smile

was caught on her lips.

'Well – there's no sense in getting you to clean the lavvy, is there? The state of you, you'd make it twice as dirty.'

'Did you win?' Martha asked brightly.

'Yes!' I couldn't stop the excitement in my voice, I felt like I was overflowing with it again. 'We won! We beat the boys. We didn't half do bad! I even scored.'

Mam's eyes widened. 'Did you now. Well – isn't that something.'

Martha's grin was so wide it looked like it could split her face in two. 'I knew it! I told you, you could do it! Isn't it great, Mam. If Dad—'

Mam turned to her sharply, her face now stern. 'Now, there's to be no mention of this to your father. Do you hear? As far as he's concerned, Hettie was just messing around with the girls today. If he hears that she played a proper game, with boys, we'd hear no end of it.'

'I won't say anything, Mam,' Martha said quietly, her expression suddenly serious.

'Good.' Mam was facing me again. She looked me up and down and shook her head quite slowly. 'Eee, I don't know, just look at the state of you. I'm going to have to get a bucket of water and rinse you off.'

I shivered at the thought, but still smiled. 'I don't mind

Mam, honest I don't. Today was amazing. The best ever. I enjoyed every second.'

'Aye, you look as if you did.' She smiled back at me, kindly. 'Do you know what? For the first time in a long while I can see colour in your cheeks. I can see the sparkle in your eyes. It's nice to see.'

'Thanks, Mam.'

She reached out and patted my arm softly. 'But even so, we mustn't say a word to your dad, all right? Not a word. If you want to carry on with this malarkey, we need to keep it to ourselves.'

'All right.' I nodded.

I didn't care. As long as I could do it again, I didn't care about keeping it a secret from Dad. All that mattered right there and then was that football had to be part of my life now. I realised that I needed it. It was a part of me that was missing.

It made me happy.

Later, Mam helped me to get washed down before Dad got home. She filled up the tin bath with some cool water and placed it in front of the low fire. I got in quick, cringing as Mam tipped more cool water from a jug down my back. The cold feeling made my entire spine contract.

'Look at the mud,' she complained. 'Did you simply roll in it?'

'I didn't intend to,' I assured her. 'But I was tackled a fair few times. They didn't spare us because we're girls.'

Mam sucked in a breath. 'It's a rough old game. You could end up getting hurt and all sorts.'

'It's not that rough, not really. There's a lot of skill involved too,' I told her. 'I've got to learn to predict the tackles better, that's all. Grace said it'll come in time.'

'Grace?' Mam said carefully. 'This is the lass behind it all, is it?'

'Aye. You'd love her, Mam – she's so confident and strong. She doesn't let anyone mess her around.'

'She sounds very interesting.' Mam stopped pouring the water and rubbed her hands on the towel that lay on the floor beside her. 'What does she make of your dad's opinions?'

I paused, my fingers circling in the water making ripples.

'I've not told her,' I said finally.

Mam nodded sadly. 'I know it must be difficult sometimes. I understand that. God knows he's not the easiest man to live with and there are some things he will never agree to.'

'Like me playing football?'

'He's not good with change. With people doing roles that aren't meant for them. The sheer thought sends him in a panic.' Mam sighed and held up the towel. I stepped into it, allowing her to curl the edges around me and wrap me up in warmth. 'He won't be the only one, Hettie. Many people will disagree with a girl playing a man's sport. They will get quite upset about it. You need to be prepared for that.'

'But you believe in equal rights,' I said. 'You said as much before now. You even said you supported the suffragettes.'

Mam sniffed and tipped her head away from me. 'Aye, that I do. It strikes me as daft that we are still living in the dark ages and that women are still regarded so poorly by others. I remember myself as a lass; how I had hopes of being a doctor when I grew up. Do you know what my dad said to me?'

'No.'

'Don't be so bloody silly That's what he said. Just like that. And he gave me a clip around my head for my troubles. Us girls aren't meant to be thinking outside our stations. We are expected to find a man and mop up after him . . .' She shook her head. 'That's all I seemed to do, mop up after my man. I had dreams, you know. Ideas. I wanted to travel. I wanted to see the countries I read about in my school books . . . America.' She sighed gently. 'How silly those dreams were, eh?'

I looked at Mam in a state of bewilderment. Then I rubbed at my mouth, not sure of the right thing to say. 'I never knew that, Mam.'

'Well – there's lots about me you don't know,' she said. 'You're like me in many ways. Independent, yet scared to face it. Keen to do different things but not quite sure what, or even how to find your own way.' She turned back to me, her eyes ablaze. 'Hettie – I want you to know that I do think it's a good thing, everything that you girls are doing. It's making those stupid, stuffy men sit up and take notice. It's making them take notice. But . . .'

'But, what?'

Her eyes grazed mine, almost as if it was too painful to look at me.

'But . . . this might not last. In the main, the majority would prefer it if us women stayed in the shadows and out of trouble. The war is distracting everyone. Our men are away fighting. When they come back, it will all go back to how it always was.'

'But Mam, it's different now. We are fighting it. We really are.'

'It's a war you'll never win, lass,' she said gently.

'They won't let you. It's been this way for hundreds of years. You won't change it now.'

I stared back at her, my eyes were filling with tears. I knew she was wrong. She had to be. The world was already changing. I could feel it. I knew.

I couldn't let my belief be broken now.

At work the following week, all talk was about the football match. You couldn't even escape from it on the factory floor. Women whispered and giggled to each other across their workbenches and the few men there had to avoid the jesting and catcalls that were thrown their way.

'Ey up! These men got beaten by a group of girls did they?' called out one large woman to a small gaggle of male apprentices. 'Reckon it could've been by much more if our ladies'd had time to put a proper team together!'

I recognised her as Peg, the woman that had shoved me in the queue on my first day. Today she had seemed far more friendly and even slapped my back as she walked past me on the shop floor.

'I hear you scored the winner, lass. Well done! A cracking result by all accounts,' she shouted.

Mr Keller soon put an end to all the shouting, telling Peg and her friends that they would be docked wages if they kept up their racket. But I noticed that he nodded at me after, in an almost-apologetic, friendly way.

'It sounds like the boys were truly beaten,' he said quietly to me, a small smile on his face. 'That's certainly interesting. But that doesn't mean work should stop. We still have a war to win here, remember?"

Then he patted my shoulder gently, before moving away.

Of course, Grace was the most excited of us all. By now, everyone in the factory knew her name and at lunchtimes she was swamped with attention – either women wanting to tell her of their possible footballing talents, or boys looking to make the odd snide comment wherever they could.

'They've certainly had their noses put out of joint,' Grace confided to me, Alice and Flo as we sat round a table on one particular break. 'George in particular seems to snarl every time I walk past.'

Alice snorted. 'I'd not bother too much about him. He's young and high-spirited. I'm sure he'll calm down in time.'

Grace pulled a face. 'Well – we've got no time for silly worries like that. I want to concentrate on the next steps. Do you girls actually think we could get a team together? A proper one, I mean.'

Flo shrugged. 'I don't see why not, Grace. We've got

enough decent players. With a bit of training and time . . . who knows?'

Grace nodded eagerly. 'That's just what I thought. Follow me.'

So we did, out into the cold yard. Some women were already gathered out there, having a quick smoke or simply breathing in the sharp air. Just along from them were some older men, managers probably. I recognised one of them as being Mr Frankland, Freddie's old boss – he was deep in conversation today with a shorter man. In the far corner, some young lads were knocking a ball around. George was with them, although he was not joining in, he was standing by the wall watching, a surly expression still etched on his face.

Grace called over to a small group of women who were chatting on the other side of the yard. I recognised them immediately. Alice Standing, Florrie, Gertie and Evelyn. They waved as we approached.

'Glad I caught you out here, ladies,' Grace said keenly. 'I thought this was a good time to run through some of my ideas.'

Gertie raised an eyebrow. 'Oh aye? And what ideas are these?'

Grace held her arms out wide. 'Us. That's what. We

have everything we need for a decent football team – especially if Flo and Alice Kell join us. We could play more games. Take on more teams.'

Evelyn giggled. 'We're already the talk of the factory. Imagine what will happen if we set up an actual team!'

'We'll be bloody amazing, that's what!' Grace replied boldly. She turned to the boys and whistled. Startled, they turned towards her.

'Pass that over, lads. Just for a moment.'

The young lad with the ball seemed to hesitate for a second and then, shrugging, he kicked the ball over to Grace, who trapped it neatly under her work boot.

'We should practise,' Grace said lightly. 'Every lunchtime. We should practise passing and working with the ball. Get ourselves used to it. We need to be stronger, work closer as a unit.'

Alice Standing was frowning. 'That's all well and good, Grace, but there were girls who played on Saturday who wouldn't be interested in forming a proper team. They wouldn't have the time.' She paused. 'And to be honest, some just aren't good enough—'

'But *we* are,' Alice Kell said, interrupting. She gestured to all of us. 'We are good enough and we can only get better.'

Every lunch it became the norm to eat our food and then step out into the yard. Grace even brought her own ball, which we kept safely in the cloakroom. We went outside even if it was freezing, or drizzling. We went outside to train and to improve. We knew it was the only way our football would get better and the results soon began to speak for themselves. Even after a few sessions out in the yard, our passes became sharper and more accurate.

Grace arranged us in our positions, with me at left wing, so we'd get used to where each player should be. She would make us dribble up the full length of the yard, avoiding obstacles she had set out for us – coats, a scarf, a battered old hat. If we touched any of the objects with the ball, or our feet, we had to go back and try again.

'It'll get you used to moving quickly with the ball,' she explained. 'It needs to feel part of you, so that the movement becomes natural.'

It was difficult doing it in skirts and corsets, though. We felt so restricted and restrained. But Grace assured us it was still good to practise.

'If you can do it dressed like this, imagine how much faster you'll be in a kit.'

I grinned at her – even the thought of that gave me a burst of energy. She was right. If we could play well dressed up as women, we'd play even stronger dressed as footballers.

It was all going well until one particular Friday. I had to admit I was feeling very tired by then. The week's shift had been hard-going and my entire body ached from being bent over the munition shells. Not only that, but I had a ripe headache from the stuffy air and the noise of the workroom. I was glad to be outside, but not thankful to be training because all I really longed for was my bed. I didn't like to say anything to Grace though. She was so excited to have us all together and training again.

There were lots of people out in the yard that afternoon. Mr Frankland was sitting on one of the benches with some boys from his office, some older women were having a gossip by the rear wall of the factory and the usual lads were playing a game of football already, taking up most of the room.

George looked up when he saw us approach. 'Oh, look who it is. The next big thing.'

Grace ignored him and simply placed her own ball on the ground; we still had some room, albeit not much.

'We can do some short passes today,' she said brightly. 'The limited space will benefit us.'

I saw George frown at this comment. It amused me that the lads seemed less focused on their own play now and instead were watching us. I think this made Grace even more determined, as she barked curt instructions at us and ordered us to pay attention.

'Hey! Why don't you play us again!'

We looked up. George was standing, arms crossed, staring right at us. A defiant look was cast across his face.

Grace hesitated. 'I'm not sure, George. We're not dressed for it.' She tugged on her dress. 'And there's limited space out here.'

A sly grin crossed George's face. He smiled smugly. 'Oh – all right. If you're too scared, then . . .'

Alice nudged Grace. 'We can have a quick game, can't we? I reckon I can still outrun that runt in my skirts.'

Flo nodded keenly. 'Yeah, c'mon. Let's have another go.'

The other girls nodded in agreement, so really there was nothing more Grace could say. She simply shrugged and smiled hesitantly.

'All right – lets have a quick game. But be mindful.

The boys might want to make a point. The ground is rock hard. If you hit the floor–'

Harry was already approaching us, the boys' ball at his feet. He held up his hands to silence Grace.

'No need to worry, Grace. Our boys won't tackle. We simply want a friendly game.'

Grace nodded in response, clearly relieved. 'That's good to know.'

We made our way to the centre of the yard; suddenly everything felt very formal. Two goals were set up at either end, using the lads' jackets. I noticed people were watching us now, gathering together to see what was about to happen. Even Mr Frankland was sitting up and looking in our direction.

Harry set the ball on the floor and he and Grace faced each other. After a brief nod of her head, the game kicked off.

There was little doubt that this time was much harder. The firm, uneven surface was difficult to move on, especially wearing work boots, and the ball often skidded and danced in unpredictable directions. The boys held possession first and it wasn't long before George was free on goal. He took the ball clumsily with his right foot and then tried to direct it towards the makeshift goal. However, instead of connecting with the ball, he somehow managed to miss completely and he ended up sprawled on the floor – his face a look of confusion – as the ball bounced away in the opposite direction.

Everyone, girls and boys, howled with laughter.

'Tripping over your own feet there, Georgie?' Harry yelled. 'Have you forgotten how to kick?'

'Quite a skill,' Flo added. 'Please show us how you did that. I'm not sure if us poor girls could replicate it!'

George pulled himself up, his face on fire. 'You lot know nothing,' he snapped back. 'You wait. I'll show you.'

And show us he did.

It wasn't long until the ball was passed to me out on the wing. I knew I didn't have much time or space to think. I had to act quickly.

I moved down the wing, faintly aware of the lumbering force of another person coming towards me. I tried to ignore it. The boys weren't going to tackle today, so I still had time. All I knew was that I needed to release the ball into our box to create our first chance.

I saw Gertie signalling for the ball and without thinking too much about it, I crossed the ball in to her.

I didn't see the goal. I later heard that it was a 'screamer', slamming into the back of the net. Unfortunately for me,

I was unable to take notice of that, because at the same time as Gertie had made contact with the ball, George had carried on running straight towards me. I saw his eyes before he connected with my leg – they looked dark and full of malice. I heard the sickening crunch as he slammed into my knee and then my body simply folded in on itself.

A rush of heat seared down my shin and then rocketed up into my thigh. My knee was a ball of fire.

I could hear the girls cheering Gertie's goal. All I wanted to do was run over and join them, but I couldn't. I could only watch as they hugged and congratulated each other. I felt no discomfort at first, just an increasing warmth, but then a searing pain began to roar behind my kneecap.

I looked up at George, still feeling stunned and ever so slightly sick. I expected to see an expression of sorrow. I expected an apology to flutter out of his lips, but instead all I saw was that cruel, smug smile slipping back on to his face.

'Not so great now, are you?' he said coldly.

'You hurt me,' I whispered, wincing as I tried to move my leg. 'You tackled when you said you wouldn't.'

'I barely touched you. It just proves you're weak, like all women.' He shook his head sadly. 'And that's why women can never play a man's sport. You're simply not capable.'

Grace flew at him.

I'd never seen anything like it – she was like a wildcat, pummelling his arms with her fists and shouting so hard that I thought her voice might break. George just stood there, taking the strikes. His expression was, by now, paler and thankfully at least his smug smirk had slipped away.

'We agreed no tackles! Why did you do that? Why did you do that to poor Hettie?' she yelled. 'You've really hurt her. Why would you do that? It's just mean . . .'

Alice and Flo were trying to ease me up. The pain shot through my leg and it was all I could do not to cry, but I wouldn't do that. Not in front of George. He'd already done enough.

'You're evil,' Grace hissed at him. 'An evil monster. That's not sport. That was an attack!'

Harry came over and rested a hand on Grace's shoulder but she shook him off, her eyes now blazing in his direction.

'Did you know he was going to do that? Did you all plan it?'

Harry looked deathly white, he stared at George in disgust. 'No. No, I didn't.'

'Why? Why would he tackle Hettie so badly, then?'

Harry looked wretched. 'I'm . . . I don't know. She's one of your best players – a risk, perhaps. George, please tell me you didn't mean to hurt her like that?'

George was now looking at his feet. 'I just wanted to teach them a lesson,' he muttered. 'They were getting too big for their boots. I just wanted to show them . . .'

'By doing this?' Grace flapped her hand towards my leg. I saw anguish in her eyes when she met my gaze. She shook her head sadly. 'Hettie can barely stand. Her knee is twice its normal size. Look at it.'

George continued to stare at the ground.

'Look at it!' Grace bellowed at him.

George very slowly looked up. His gaze drifted for a second, before settling on my raised skirt. My knee was clear for him to see. Huge, sore and red. I noticed how he swallowed hard and licked his lips.

'I never meant . . .'

He ran his hand through his hair and looked in turn at his teammates, who were staring back at him with a mixture of despair and disgust.

'I never meant to hurt her. Not that bad, like.'

'Well, you did!' Grace snapped. 'Out of temper and sheer jealousy, you did this.'

She reached forward. 'Come with me, Hettie. I'll take

you to Mr Keller. You need to go home and rest. But I'll tell you now, you'll not lose your wages for this. I'll make sure of that.'

I tried to put weight on my leg, but the pain so was overwhelming that I fell to the floor screaming, tears biting in my eyes. I didn't want to remain on the floor, being watched by everyone. Slowly, gritting my teeth, I pulled myself to my feet in front of all the men. I wanted them to see that they couldn't keep me down. Grace took my hand, her grip was warm and reassuring in mine. She smiled at me hesitantly and squeezed my fingers.

'I'm so sorry, Hettie.'

'You . . .' I gasped, grimacing in pain. 'You . . . have nothing to be sorry for.'

'But this was my idea. All of this. I'd never have let us play them again if I'd known—'

'You couldn't have known,' I interrupted. 'This was George's fault. No one else's.'

But . . . if I had been sharper, quicker . . . If I hadn't been so tired. Maybe I would've predicted what he was going to do . . .? Did I make it too easy for him?'

'Can I help at all, ladies? I saw what happened. What an awful thing.'

Mr Frankland was approaching us, looking concerned

and rather flustered. Grace led me, hobbling painfully, towards him.

'Mr Frankland,' she breathed. 'Would it be possible for Hettie to be sent home? She got awfully injured. It was all George's fault, not hers.'

'I saw everything,' he replied sternly. 'Of course she can go home. She cannot continue to work in this state. I will have a word with her supervisor and ensure she is not docked any money. I'll also have a word with that lad's boss about his behaviour out there . . .'

'Thank you,' we both muttered.

Grace squeezed my hand. 'I'll take you. I'll help you get home. You can't walk on your own.'

'But you'll lose money if you're late back!'

'It doesn't matter. It's more important that I see you home.'

I didn't argue any further. The pain in my leg was too much. I needed to support myself on Grace's sturdy body to even stand half a chance of making it back in one piece.

'I can't believe he did it,' I muttered, as we moved out of the gate.

'I can,' Grace said. 'There's many like him that want to take the likes of us down. I'm only sad that he succeeded with you, dear Hettie.'

A cold feeling surged in my stomach.

What if he *had* succeeded? Did this mean I'd never play again?

I turned away from Grace. I didn't want her to see the tears that were building up.

I'd only just found something I was good at, something I enjoyed. Was it really about to be taken away from me?

'I'm so sorry,' Grace said again.

I couldn't answer her this time. But in my head, all I could think was, *please don't be.*

Don't let this be the end.

Mam applied a hot compress to my swollen knee and said nothing at all, her lips firmly pressed together and her cheeks flushed pink. But Dad – Dad, who had returned from work in a fouler mood than ever – had a lot to say on the subject. I was left wondering why I had hated his silences so much. They were so much better than his bursts of anger.

'I told you,' he scolded, in the direction of Mam, not me. 'Look at her. What a state she is, with her skirt all dirty and a knee twice the size of the other one. What good will she be round the house now, eh? No good at all.'

He was talking as if I wasn't in the room; he could barely look at me. It was as if I had committed some awful crime – although I suppose in some ways I had. I hadn't listened to him.

'She'll still go to work,' Dad continued. 'Even if she has to hop there on one leg, she'll go. It'll never be right again, you know. Not a knee. Not an injury like that.

I can tell you that now. She'll be lucky not to have a limp – or long-lasting pain.'

I didn't bother to tell Dad that I had every intention of still going to the factory, somehow. I had to see the girls.

His words stung me, though. I was terrified by what he was saying might happen. My knee really was hurting a treat and the swelling didn't look good at all. Mam had already asked one of the neighbours, Mrs Taylor, to take a look at it when I first got home. Mrs Taylor had some experience with nursing and knew about such things. She took one look at my leg and tutted under her breath.

'That looks nasty. It really does. I reckon you've sprained the kneecap.' She shook her head slowly, as if telling me off. 'You can't be doing any silly business on this leg, now. You'll need rest, and lots of it.'

'I wasn't doing any silly business,' I muttered and Mam shot me a warning look. She obviously didn't want the street to know how I got injured.

And now Dad was so wound-up he could barely keep still. He kept pacing the room.

'I thought it were a one-off, that morning on the rec. You both told me it was just a kick-around and nothing more!'

'We were larking about in the yard on our break,' I said. 'It was an accident, that's all.'

Dad snorted. 'Are you telling me a woman did this to you?'

I flinched. I knew the intention behind his words. He thought no woman was capable of playing football properly or being strong enough to injure me like this. But the truth was, none of our girls would have made such a reckless or clumsy tackle.

'A boy did it,' I admitted, not seeing the point of lying any longer. 'We were playing the boys.'

Mam groaned out loud. 'Hettie – what did I tell you—'

'You were playing the boys?' Dad boomed. 'Well, this gets even better. Tell me the truth – were you playing the boys that morning on the rec too?'

I nodded meekly. Mam shot me an angry look but I ignored her.

Dad chuckled, but it was a cold, hollow sound. 'So let me get this right. My daughter was outside, in front of everyone, pretending to play at football—'

'I wasn't pretending—'

'Enough!' He held up his hand. 'Have you any idea what this looks like? People will be talking. They will be saying things about you, about our family . . .'

'We beat them though, Dad,' I said, tears swelling in my eyes. 'We beat them. We're good. We could be even better if we keep practising.'

'And who's been filling your head with this nonsense?' he snapped back.

I thought of Grace, how she helped me to the door and offered to stay with me. How she was so worried for me that her own face was pale with anguish. I thought of how she had squeezed my hand tight in hers and told me that I was a great footballer. That she thought *I* was great.

'No one has, Dad,' I replied.

He stared at me for a second, his eyes as cool as water. 'Well – it doesn't matter now, does it. Fate has intervened. It's stopped you making a fool of yourself any more.'

I bent my head, sadness overwhelming me. 'I want to keep playing, Dad.'

His laugh was short and cruel. 'Well, you can't now. Not with a knackered knee like that. You've brought this on yourself, Hettie. You deserve it for your wicked behaviour and lies. This is your punishment.'

Almost as if he could sense my thoughts, Dad continued to pace. His angry expression had lifted a little, but his words were still brutal.

'This is the end of the road for you and football,

young lady, and a good job too. You need to forget this nonsense and stay away from those women.'

I lowered my gaze, all thoughts of my knee forgotten – for now, the pain seemed deeply rooted in my chest instead.

It was all over.

I'd never play again.

Martha pressed against me in bed that night. Her clammy hand reached for mine and I pulled it towards me, holding it close to my chest. It felt nice there. I was facing away from her so that she couldn't see my tear-streaked face, but it was hard to control the sobs that racked my body. I felt so tired and so, so lost – like I was spinning out of control.

How was it fair that I had found something good, something exciting – only to have it snatched away from me? Maybe Dad was right. Maybe I was a bad person who deserved this.

But I didn't know what bad thing I had done to cause myself this much hurt.

'I wish Freddie were here,' I whispered under my breath.

I stared at his bed, still freshly made, still neat and tidy. I imagined him sitting on top of it, smiling gently. What would he say to me?

Chin up, Hettie. It'll work out. It always does . . .

Or, *Don't listen to Dad, you know what he gets like . . .*

But I needed to hear Freddie say the words himself. I needed him more than ever and he wasn't here. He was God knows where. I didn't even know if he was still alive.

I sobbed again.

Martha lifted her head behind me.

'Don't cry, Hettie.'

'I'm sorry. I really am. I can't seem to stop.'

'Is it your knee? Is it still hurting?'

'It is, but that's not what's making me cry.'

'What is it, then? Do you want me to fetch Mam?'

I was thankful that Martha had been out playing earlier. She hadn't heard the angry words that Dad had said to me and I didn't want her to know. There was no point in us both being upset.

'I'm just sad, Marth,' I said. 'I don't think I can play football again.'

'Not ever?'

'Well – I don't know, but certainly not for some time. I need to rest my leg. Mrs Taylor said it might never be the same. Knees are quite tricky to heal.'

Martha sighed. 'But she might be wrong?'

'She could be. I don't know.'

'You could still get better, Hettie. You don't know for sure.'

I couldn't answer. All of my thoughts felt so jumbled and confused. I was too overwhelmed with sadness and disappointment to consider anything else.

'You just have to wait and see, don't you?' Martha said, yawning. She snuggled back in beside me. 'Like Mam always says, tomorrow is a new day.'

'It is,' I replied quietly.

It'd be a new day all right – but a much bleaker one.

I left for work earlier than usual the next day on account of my knee. Hobbling on the cobblestones proved difficult, but Mam had tightly bound my injury so I could bear a little weight on it at least. However, I could tell by Flo and Alice's faces as they met me on the corner that I must've looked a right sight.

'Ouch, Hettie, that looks so sore,' Flo said, rushing over to take my arm. 'Should you even be walking on it?'

'My dad said I have to put up with it,' I muttered, pushing my sweaty hair away from my face. 'It was my fault for playing.'

Alice tutted loudly. 'And I suppose you chose to hurt your knee, did you?'

'You were lucky not to break your leg,' Flo added, peering down at it. 'That George deserves a slap around the head to bring some sense to him.'

Alice sighed. 'Don't be too harsh on the lad. One of my brothers knows him. He gets a lot of hassle from his dad about not being a good enough football player.'

'Well, that would explain why he hates being beaten by girls,' Flo replied. 'But even so, that doesn't excuse his behaviour.'

'If his dad is hard on him, he might not be thinking straight,' I said, wincing again from the pain my knee. 'I should know about that, after all.'

'I'm sorry, but your dad does sound a bit mardy,' Alice said. 'It was hardly your fault.'

'Dad just blames me for playing in the first place. He never wanted me to.' I flinched as we moved forward. 'Dad says that football isn't proper for women. He's always thought like that.'

Flo snorted. 'Well, he's not alone there – half the lads in the factory think the girls were wrong to play in the first place.' Her eyes flashed as she shook her head defiantly. 'I don't understand their thinking, I really don't. Why can't a girl play if she's good enough? What difference does it make?'

'Our lads don't like to feel threatened,' Alice scoffed. 'God help us if we end up being better than them at something.'

'Think how they'll feel when me and Alice join the team!' Flo said. 'We'll be a force to be reckoned with.'

I looked up, the pain in my knee momentarily forgotten. 'Are you joining? Really?'

Alice grinned. 'I went and spoke to Grace at her house last night. After getting involved with the training, we both knew for sure that we wanted to be part of it.'

'That's the best news,' I said and then grimaced as pain shot through me again.

Alice squeezed my arm gently. 'I'm sorry about your knee, Hettie, honestly I am. You looked so good out there. I only hope you can play again soon.'

'Even if I could, I doubt my dad would let me.'

'That's so unfair,' grumbled Flo.

'It's the way it is with my dad,' I said softly. 'He thinks it's important for everyone to know their place. He seems to think if that changes . . . I dunno . . . society will crumble or something. So the women should stay at home. The men should go to work . . . you know . . . It makes him feel better when everything is as it should be.'

Alice stopped walking and looked at me, a tiny frown on her face. 'But it's different now, isn't it? We *have* to go to work. Our men are fighting. We need to fill in where they left off.'

'People are waking up,' Flo said. 'Look at the suffragettes. Women are demanding more.'

'I know,' I agreed. 'But men like my dad don't understand. I don't think they ever will.'

Alice snorted. 'Well, they're going to have to soon or they'll be left behind.'

I was surprised to see Mr Connor and Mr Frankland on the shop floor as we approached our workbenches. Annoyingly, they were standing right by where I worked. I tried to hobble past without making too much of a fuss. The last thing I needed was to be sent home again because I was unfit to work. I was bound to have my money docked this time. I knew how much Mam and Dad needed my wages now that Freddie was away. I didn't need for Dad to be any angrier with me than he already was.

Fortunately, it looked like the two men were deep in discussion, looking at some plans that Mr Frankland was holding up. I made a bold attempt to walk as normally as I could to my workstation, hoping that they wouldn't notice me, but as soon as I put weight back on my gammy leg, the pain shot through me again. It was all I could do not to curse out loud. Instead I winced and paused for a moment or two. Unfortunately, it was a moment or two too long.

'Are you all right there, young lady? Is your leg still troubling you?'

I looked up. Mr Frankland had folded up his plans and was looking at me with a curious but quite kindly expression.

'Oh – I'm fine . . .' I stammered. 'It'll be fine once I get going.'

I attempted to move again, but the pain was shocking and I found myself reaching out for the nearest bench to regain balance. This really wasn't good enough. I had to start work now, or I'd be in trouble.

I glanced up at Mr Connor waiting for him to shout, but instead a small smile was creeping up on his face.

'So, how did you hurt yourself?' he said, one eyebrow raising. 'I heard it was out in the yard, yesterday?'

I wasn't sure what to say. Panic flooded me. Was I about to get a telling-off? 'Er . . . yes, sir.'

'Hmmm.' He rubbed his chin and then turned to Mr Frankland. 'And this is the result of the football match you were telling me about?'

I stared at both of them blankly. I was worried that Mr Connor might be angry. It was so difficult to tell from his expression.

Mr Frankland laughed. It was loud and hearty and startled me a little. 'Oh, come on, girl! Don't look so worried! You're not in trouble, in fact, you girls are the talk of the factory. It's all the lads in my office have been talking about.' He addressed Mr Connor. 'Yesterday, I was watching them taking on some of the lads outside. They gave the boys quite a game, I can tell you. I would've liked to have seen more.'

Mr Connor snorted. 'Well, that means nothing. Those boys have lost nearly every game they've played this season. I expect my seventy-year-old mother could beat them in her carpet slippers.'

Mr Frankland's eyes twinkled. 'That, I would like to see!'

I bowed my head a little, feeling the warmth in my cheeks. 'It was just a little game, nothing much, but I did twinge my knee a bit.' I paused, testing my weight on it again. The joint burnt fiercely under the pressure and I shuddered. Would it ever stop hurting? 'I'll be all right today if I could perhaps sit down while working . . .'

'Sit down? This is a factory, not a rest room.' Mr Connor looked frustrated now. 'Look, I've got no time to waste on an injured worker. You'll simply have to go home and come back when you are fully fit and able. I can't afford to pay you for another missed day though.' His eyes drilled into mine. 'Maybe next time you'll consider your situation before playing games that were never meant for girls.'

'Yes, sir,' I muttered, feeling about two feet tall.

'Ah, now, David,' Mr Frankland reached forward and touched Mr Connor's arm. 'Let's not be too harsh on the girl. I saw what happened. That young boy George was quite rough with her. You were very unfortunate, weren't you . . . ah . . .' He stammered, obviously unsure of my name.

'Hettie Blakeford,' I told him and he nodded.

'Blakeford?' His eyes widened. 'Did your brother work for me?'

'Yes.' I smiled back at him. 'Freddie. He signed up for the cause a few months back. The last we heard, he was in France.'

Mr Frankland's face grew grave. 'Ah, well. I hope that he's safe and well. He's a good lad, that one. A hard worker, and honest too.' He turned to Mr Connor. 'He was the boy I told you about before, the one that wanted to be a photographer. Very talented, actually.'

Mr Connor looked unsure. 'Er . . . Right, I do seem to remember . . .'

'He really wants to do that still. He's saving up for a camera and everything,' I said keenly. 'When he gets home, once this war is won, he hopes to take it up for good.'

Mr Frankland nodded slowly. 'That sounds like a very sensible plan.'

Both men stood there for a moment, looking at me, and an uneasy silence fell between us. I got the squirmy feeling in my stomach that I always got when I felt uncomfortable or worried about a situation. It was like having a thousand worms wriggling around in my belly.

'So . . . I should go, then?' I said finally, feeling defeated.

I thought of Mam, and what her reaction would be if I walked through the door now. She'd pretend not to care about the loss of money, but I know she'd be worried really. And what would Dad say? He'd likely scold me and say that he told me so – but would there also be a chance he would be even angrier with me. Maybe he would be unable to forgive me. I didn't think I could stand it if that were the case. It was bad enough already that I felt such crushing disappointment about my injury, I didn't also want to feel like I'd let my parents down.

'I don't think you should go home,' Mr Frankland

said suddenly. 'I think you should come and work in my office instead.'

'Alfred, I hardly think–'

Mr Frankland flapped Mr Connor's objections away. 'Why not? We are struggling as it is, now that Johnny Armstrong has been called up. I could do with someone to help me with telephone enquiries, letter typing, that sort of thing. It's all desk work, so there'll be no need for standing. Do you think you could do that, Hettie?'

'I–I think I could try,' I stammered, trying to fight back the overwhelming feelings of relief and gratitude.

'Well, there we go then,' Mr Frankland said smoothly. 'Mr Connor, you no longer have a lame worker and I have an eager and willing apprentice.'

Mr Connor shook his head slowly. 'Well – I can't see it working, but if you insist.'

'I insist.'

'Thank you, Mr Frankland!' I said brightly. 'I really will try my best.'

'I know you will,' he replied kindly. 'And don't thank me, thank your brother. He's the reason I'm willing to give you a go. If you're even a tiny bit like him, I reckon you're worth a shot.'

I wanted to say that it was my dream to be compared

to my brother, that I had spent most of my life aspiring to be just like him. But instead I smiled gratefully and thanked him, wondering if he had any idea how much his words meant to me.

It felt like the first glimmer of hope in a very long time.

Mr Frankland's office was smaller and darker than the loud factory floor. It was also a lot quieter. A few younger lads, Mr Frankland's apprentices, were leaning over a huge drawing board in the corner of the room. Mr Frankland had a small desk at the back, which he took me over to. It was large and mainly uncluttered and he sat so that he could see out of the window.

He gestured for me to sit down on the small chair opposite him and then chortled softly as he saw my eyes flick to the view beside him.

'That's why I like my office the best,' he said. 'I can see right out over the yard. In fact, many a time I've sat here, pretending to get on with my business, but instead I'm distracted by matters elsewhere. Like, for example, some young ladies kicking a ball around out there.'

'Really, sir?' I said. 'You've watched us before?'

'Indeed. That's why I came outside, to watch more closely. I must say, there are some talented women here.'

I nodded. 'There really are, sir.'

'You included.' He smiled. 'And please don't call me sir, Hettie. Mr Frankland will do nicely.'

I nodded politely.

'You seemed very talented when I saw you play the other day,' he continued.

The familiar ice-cool feeling swamped my stomach. I didn't want him to talk about my football. What was the point now? Bitterness snapped at me.

'Anyway,' Mr Frankland said, obviously sensing my mood. 'It's a nice spot up here.'

I had to agree. I couldn't imagine having an office of my own, let alone one with such a view. Even our bedroom window at home was small and poky and simply looked out at the endless chimney pots that lined our street. I glanced at Mr Frankland, with his smart suit, his good manners and his neatly combed hair and I tried to picture the type of house that he must live in. I told myself that it had to be grand, rather like the man himself.

I shifted in my seat, feeling inadequate and out of place in this large, plush office, and quite by accident I knocked my knee on the leg of the desk. It wasn't even very hard, but the pain still shot through my leg. I flinched immediately, trying not to cry out, and rubbed my leg furiously in an attempt to remove the pain.

'Are you quite all right?' Mr Frankland asked, leaning forward. 'You look quite pale. I can fetch you a tea before I run through the work. Would that help? Is your knee causing you pain again?'

'A little,' I admitted. 'But I'll be ok. I promise.'

Mr Frankland nodded. 'Well – if you're sure. I like the idea of having a new assistant up here with me, but not one that might pass out in pain.'

'I won't, sir, I mean . . . Mr Frankland,' I promised.

At least, I hoped not.

'It was quite a knock,' he said softly. 'You were lucky to be able to get up again. I've seen many men laid up on their backs with such an injury.'

'It was a bad tackle,' I grumbled, not able to stop myself. 'It was very late. George came charging in on me before I could stop it.'

Mr Frankland sighed. 'A sign of frustration, I'd wager.'

'Perhaps.'

He sat forward again, his hands clasped in front of him. 'In fact, there was another reason why I was keen to have you work with me.' His cheeks reddened a little and he rubbed his chin as if nervous. 'There is something else I would like your help with.'

'Oh.' I stared back at him confused. How would a

kid from Spa Road ever be able to help a man like this? Was he feeling all right?

'I'd like to get involved with the team. The women's team,' he said. 'I made mention of it before, to another girl, but she just laughed it off. I suppose she thought I wasn't being serious. But I am. I think I could really help.'

'You do?' I paused, uncertain. 'How?'

Mr Frankland nodded as if he expected that question. 'Well, obviously I enjoy the game. I've also seen how well other women's teams have done elsewhere, in other factories. People underestimate them, but they play very well.' His voice lowered a little. 'Also, like I said, I've seen some of the women out there in the yard. I've seen how they move with the ball. Many of them are as good as any man I've seen.'

'I have to agree with you on that matter,' I said.

'Also, I'm a good manager. I'm organised. I can motivate. I can get the best out of people, I really do believe that.'

'Those things are important,' I agreed. 'But . . . well, Grace is good at managing the girls . . . they respect her.'

'And so they should,' he replied firmly. 'But all good teams need a manager. Grace, and players like her, are still fundamental to the running of the team – but I'd like Grace to have the time to concentrate on playing and helping the girls. The team will thrive from guidance, support and funding. That's where I come in.'

'Funding?'

'For proper kits and boots.' He paused. 'And I think I can negotiate with the likes of Preston North End football club to use their pitches.'

I shook my head. 'But Mr Frankland . . . with respect, you are quite alone in thinking this. Most people won't want to help a women's football team – not when there's more important concerns out there.'

Surprisingly Mr Frankland beamed at my comment. 'Ah! But that's where you're wrong, Hettie. I think people *will* change their minds. I think people will see just how good teams like the Dick, Kerr Girls can be . . .'

'But why will people suddenly pay attention now?' I said sharply. 'I'm not sure they will.'

'Because there is great need for this now.' He continued smiling at me. 'Most men are away fighting. There is an opportunity for our women to step in and entertain the crowds. Maybe they can do more than that. Maybe this could be the start of something wonderful . . .'

I sat back in my chair, quite bemused by his excitement. 'You really want to do this, don't you, Mr Frankland?' I said.

'Yes. Yes, I do.'

'But I still don't understand . . . How can I help you?'

His eyes fixed on mine, bright and alert. 'I want you on board with me. Helping with the organising. Supporting the girls. Being my number two.' He smiled kindly. 'It will mean a lot to the team to have you with them and while you're recovering, it will give you a chance to still be involved.'

I stared down at my feet. 'But that's the thing. I might never recover, with this type of injury. There's no knowing.'

'But you could still be *involved*, Hettie. Wouldn't that be a wonderful thing? You could still be a part of the team's journey.'

I continued looking at my feet. Thoughts buzzed around my head. I thought of the girls, of course – of Grace and Alice and Flo. They were so important to me already. And still, Dad's words rang in my ears. This journey wasn't meant for me. The accident had just proved as much.

Girls like me were never meant to be part of changing things. It was all too big, too unreachable for someone like me. My destiny was already set in stone.

I looked up again and this time held Mr Frankland's kindly gaze.

'I'm sorry, sir,' I said firmly. 'But I'm not able to help you with that.'

I wish it could've been different. I really did.

But I had accepted my fate.

Later, I hobbled into the house, keen to get to my bed and rest. I was also hoping that Mam would be pleased to hear that I was working in an office just like our Freddie. In her eyes, it would be the start of something good. New beginnings.

I only wished I felt more cheerful about it. All I kept thinking about was Mr Frankland's offer and my refusal. But I knew I had done the right thing. Nobody in the team would want an injured girl hanging about, not really, and what was the point of making Dad any angrier with me? I had to move on.

But as I stepped through the dimly lit passageway to the tightly drawn front room, I realised something was amiss. My stomach plummeted. Martha was sat at the table, her legs crossed in front of her, her face all serious and pale. Mam was sitting on the big chair facing the door, but her head was turned away from me. And Dad . . . Dad was back from work already, standing in the centre of the room, clutching a piece of paper. I knew what it was without looking it.

A telegram.

A cold feeling crept over me.

'Freddie,' I gasped. 'It's Freddie, isn't it?'

Mam lifted her head towards me, and I could see where the tears had left trails on her red skin.

'Yes . . .' she stammered. 'We've finally heard. Hettie – we've finally heard.'

And then she began to cry.

'What is it? What's happened?'

My words came out in a flurry as I rushed forward and took Mam's hands in mine. I wanted to stop her tears. I wanted her to look at me and tell me clearly what had happened.

I just needed to know.

Mam squeezed my hands tight. Her warmth bled through to me.

'Hettie, love. I'm so sorry,' she said quickly. 'I'm so sorry – it's all the emotion. It overtook me. I think you've got the wrong idea.'

'What?' I shook my head, confused.

'Freddie isn't dead,' my dad said flatly. 'Although he may as well be.'

'What do you mean?' I tugged my hands away from Mam and turned to face Dad. 'What do you mean by that?'

'He's coming home. Injured, they say.' He shook his head slowly. 'Gassed. He was gassed in the trenches. We don't know how badly – I've heard such bad things from other folk, bad, bad things . . .'

Dad screwed up the telegram in his hands. I noticed how grey his skin was, how he couldn't meet my eyes. He seemed different somehow, frailer.

'Gassed?' I repeated the word. It sounded scary and wrong in my mouth. 'What does that even mean?'

'What do you think it means, lass?' Dad snapped. 'That gas is a weapon. It gets into your chest, into your lungs, and rots them away. It stops you breathing–'

'Don't talk like that!' Mam interrupted, her eyes blazing. 'We don't know anything. We don't know how bad he is yet.'

'Such a young lad,' Dad appeared to be talking to himself now. 'I told him not to go, fighting some fruitless war, for what? What will he have now? Who will help him now?' He shook his head. 'Not this government, that's for sure. They don't help the likes of us. He's ruined his entire life.'

No one seemed to notice Martha was quietly sobbing, I hobbled over to her and scooped her into a hug. 'Sssh, now. It'll be all right,' I soothed.

'But Dad says Freddie is badly hurt . . .' she gulped.

'We don't know yet.' I turned to Dad again. 'Did the telegram say anything about his injuries?'

'No – just that he's coming home.'

'There. See. We know nothing,' I said firmly. 'We will have to wait and see. But this is Freddie we are talking about. Freddie is strong. Freddie is a fighter.'

And he promised me he would return. He said that he would return home and that he would be as right as rain.

I had to believe him.

I dreamt of Freddie that night. He was home again, sitting with us in the front room. His smile was as bright as the fire that Mam had just lit. Dad was there too, sat on the large chair in the corner. His frown had gone and his face looked softer and kinder. A face that I hadn't seen for so long now.

'I told you I'd be all right,' Freddie said calmly. 'I told you.'

Then he smiled, a bright gaping smile. But instead of teeth, all I could see was blood. It coated his mouth and spilt out over his lips.

'I told you,' he said again.

He started coughing and his eyes were wild with fear as he gripped his throat.

'I told you . . .' he gasped. 'I told you—'

I woke up, a sharp breath catching in my throat.

Martha stirred beside me. 'What is it?' she murmured.

I pulled her closer to my body, breathed in her hot, salty scent.

'It's nothing, Martha. Nothing at all,' I whispered.

Sleep would not come back to me, though. I lay for ages in the dark, staring blankly at the shadows on the wall, trying hard to rid myself of that last image of Freddie.

But all I could see was his blood as he struggled to breathe.

The morning was much brighter, even though there was still a sharp chill in the air. I woke feeling groggy after finally managing a few hours of sleep and I was thankful to leave my bed.

I tried to ignore the tension that was still hanging over our house like a dark cloud. Mam was busy in the kitchen, but I saw that she had left the telegram out on the table. Her eyes kept flicking over to it, as if it would suddenly give her more information.

'We should have more word soon,' she said softly. 'We should know more.'

There was no sign of Dad. I assumed he had left for work early, but I could feel the shadow of his fear lingering in the room. Even Martha was quieter than usual, and she looked ghostly pale as she sat spooning mouthfuls of grey porridge into her mouth.

'It'll be OK, Mam,' I said, gently kissing her rouged cheek. I could smell the fresh powder on her skin. Even in crisis, Mam had to be made up and have her hair shiny and pinned back. It was only the far-away expression in her eyes that gave away her true feelings.

The walk to work wasn't quite as bad this time. My knee was less swollen by now and I could bear to put some weight on it. Pain still flared behind the kneecap though – a constant reminder that I couldn't allow myself to do too much on it.

I was surprised to see Flo and Alice waiting for me on the corner of the street as I'd assumed that they would have gone ahead, not wanting to be made late by my hobbling.

'Here she is!' Flo flung her arm around me. 'How are you holding up?'

'Not too bad.' I lifted my leg a little to show them. 'It's healing well enough, but it's still very stiff.'

'You'll soon be playing football again.'

I froze. The empty feeling inside of me seemed to grow larger still. I couldn't bear to look at Alice's eager face, so I quickly looked away.

'I don't think so. Not now. My time is done.'

Flo released her arm and looked at me in alarm. 'Oh, Hettie, don't say that! Surely you don't want to stop? Not now me and Alice are involved.'

'Oh, it's not that.' I paused, gathering my thoughts a little. 'I just don't think this is for me. It was fun while it lasted. I think the injury was a sign that I shouldn't be playing.'

My voice broke. The two girls were staring at me curiously, so I carried on.

'Like I said before, my dad doesn't approve at all and I have bigger things to worry about now.' I bit the inside of my lip, not wanting to say the words. 'My brother, Freddie, he's coming home. They say he's injured but we don't know how bad.'

'Oh.' Alice stared at me wide-eyed; her hand reached up to touch my shoulder. 'Oh, Hettie. I'm so sorry. But he's coming home, right? That has to be a good thing? Is he going to Moor Park?'

Moor Park was the local military hospital where a lot of our injured men had ended up.

'We think so,' I said. 'Mam is trying to find out more.'

Alice sighed wearily. 'This war. It really does you in, doesn't it?'

My gaze drifted towards my feet. I couldn't quite look her in the eye. I thought of her own brother again and how she must be feeling.

'Aye – it does,' I muttered. 'I'm so sorry, Alice – about Tom. I go on about Freddie and all the time—'

Alice held out her hand to stop me. 'It's all right, lass. We all have our worries. It's so bleedin' hard. Just because I'm hurting, it doesn't mean I don't understand.'

'We have each other,' Flo said firmly, looping her arm in mine. 'We must remember that. We have each other to help us through these hard times.'

'The Dick, Kerr Girls,' Alice said brightly, pressing her body close to mine.

'The Dick, Kerr Girls,' I repeated. But the words felt hollow.

How could I call myself a Dick, Kerr Girl now? I was nothing. I was an outsider again, like I always had been. A person with little purpose.

I blinked back the tears, unable to say anything else.

Would I ever belong anywhere? Or would I always feel this way?

The morning in the office went quickly as I busied myself answering Mr Frankland's many telephone calls and filing much of his overflowing paperwork. To be honest, it was nice to keep myself busy and stop my mind wandering to Freddie and the overwhelming disappointment of my injury.

At lunch, I excused myself and made my way to the huge dinner hall. The sights and sounds of this boisterous place were surprisingly comforting; they helped to take over the negative thoughts that were burrowed deep in my mind.

It was good to find Alice, Flo and Grace in the queue, waiting to be served. They keenly called me over.

'No – don't you mind her, she's not pushing in,' Grace said loudly to the sour-looking girl stood behind her. 'This is Hettie. She's one of us. And she's hurt her leg, poor lass. I'll not have her standing around on it for too long.'

Grace smiled at me warmly, but I saw the dark smudges of shadow under her eyes and the heaviness of her movement. I wondered whether she'd had enough sleep.

'How's your knee?' Grace asked me gently. 'I hope it's not too painful? And what's this I hear about you working with old Alfred Frankland?'

I nodded. 'I am at the moment. It's not so bad.'

'I'll bet. Anything beats standing on your feet for hours on end filling chuffin' shells.' She nudged Flo. 'I reckon we'll end up bright canary yellow like Peggy.'

'I'd better not. Yellow's not my colour,' Flo shot back brightly.

Grace smiled back, but said nothing more. She seemed distracted.

'I like Mr Frankland,' I said, moving closer and dropping my voice. 'And he likes you – the team, I mean. He's really interested in it.'

'Really?' Alice raised an eyebrow. 'How, exactly?'

'He'd like to help out.' I saw both girl's eyes widen in disbelief, so I continued. 'Honestly, he really wants to get involved. He thinks with the right support the Dick, Kerr team could do really well. Better than anyone else, in fact.'

'Does he now?' Flo breathed. 'Did you hear that, Gracie? Mr Frankland thinks he can take us on. Isn't that great?'

Grace shrugged. 'Yes, I suppose it is,' she said. 'Although, to be honest, I'm not sure whether it matters any more to me.'

And then she turned her back on both of us.

Alice pulled a face at me. It was an 'I don't know what's up with her' sort of face. Not knowing what to do back, I smiled shyly. I wondered if Grace was feeling as miserable as me and if so, why. We remained in the queue in silence and I was grateful when we were finally served and were able to sit down. The tension was bothering me and my leg was really beginning to throb again.

It was only once we'd sat down, at a table far away from everyone else, that Alice was able to nudge Grace firmly in the side. Flo was frowning at her a little.

'What was that all about just now? About the team not mattering. Having a girls' team means everything to you, you've said so often enough.'

'Aye, it does, it really does.' Grace lowered her head slowly, not looking at either of us. 'But I guess some things matter more.'

Her words drilled through me. Had she heard what I'd said earlier this morning? Had Alice and Flo told her?

'Like what?' Alice snapped. 'All I'm hearing today is that other things matter more than the team. It seems to be a repeating theme.'

I stared down at my dinner, my cheeks blazing. I could tell Alice was irritated, but I quickly realised it couldn't be because of me. I was no use to anyone now.

But Grace, on the other hand . . . Grace was vital to the team.

They needed Grace.

'Other things – like my husband.' Grace looked up again. Her eyes were bright and clear. 'Like my beloved.

Remember him? He left to go to fight in the war, only it turns out that the war took the fight out of him – what's left of him, anyway.'

A cold chill slipped down my spine. I almost gasped. Oh no, not Jimmy. Not him, too.

'What's happened, Grace?' Alice whispered.

'They say he's been captured, that's what,' Grace said. 'Taken to a prisoner of war camp somewhere.' She shook her head and her soft waves bounced gently with the movement. 'So, excuse me for not being excited about the team, but you could say I have more pressing matters to worry about.'

And then with a sudden little gasp, she jumped up and ran out of the dinner hall.

'Should we go after her?' I asked.

Alice shook her head sadly. 'No – I don't think that would be wise. Grace needs some time to herself. She's got a lot to think about, poor lass. I just hope she didn't think I was too hard on her – going on about football.'

Flo touched Alice's hand gently. 'Grace understands. Normally she's the one nattering on about it. Her head's all over the place, that's all.'

I nodded. I knew the feeling well now.

Alice leant forward and nudged Flo. 'What's wrong

with you? You've got a daft expression on your face.'

'Have I?' Flo sat back and smiled sweetly. 'Sorry, I was miles away.'

'I could tell. What were you dreaming about then?' Her grin broadened. 'Not some fella, eh?'

'No!' Flo's grin broadened. 'Not this time. I was thinking about what Hettie was saying. About Mr Frankland and his offer to manage the team. Don't you think it's a good idea?'

Alice seemed to consider this for a moment. 'Well, I know I for one would love to get a proper team off the ground. I think we have enough talented players . . .'

'We do, don't we?' Flo said keenly.

Alice nodded. 'I'm sure of it. Actually, I've had a number of girls come up and ask me if we are going to play again and if they could be included.' She paused and sipped her drink. 'We might have to run trials – pick the best ones.'

'It does sound exciting,' I said, trying to keep the jealousy from my voice. I only wished I could take part in those trials.

'It is.' Alice sat up straighter, her face brightening. 'I mean, just look at the team that beat the boys that weekend and we weren't even prepared. We hadn't trained together or anything.'

'Do you really think Mr Frankland could help us?" Flo asked.

Alice nodded slowly. 'I don't know Mr Frankland that well, but I have heard he has an interest in sporting matters.' She drummed her fingers on the table, her gaze drifting off in thought. 'It would be good to have someone else on board. Someone to give us direction and support.'

'He is very keen,' I said.

I didn't tell them that he'd asked me to help. What would be the point? Alice and Flo would act all nice about it, but they didn't need me in the shadows. I was a spare part now. Nothing more.

Flo was buzzing with excitement. 'Alice, this could be the start of something amazing.'

'I know.' Alice's eyes were glistening, but then she hesitated. 'I know this could be amazing, Flo, I do. But we need to speak to Grace. We need to make sure she is all right with all of this. It's so important to her. We shouldn't leave her out of any decisions.'

Flo nodded. 'Of course.'

Alice seemed sadder now. 'I just hope Grace still wants to be a part of it. This is her team, after all.'

Mam received a follow-up letter about Freddie later that same week. I saw her clutching it in her hand when I came home from work. I kicked off my boots and joined her in the warm kitchen, where she was sitting at the table with the papers spread out in front of her. There was no sign of Martha, who I assumed was in our bedroom, nor Dad, who I assumed was at the pub.

I was glad for both.

'What does it say?' I said softly, trying to ignore the dip and swirl inside my stomach.

Mam's fingers were delicately tracing the words, as if she could read them through touch alone. She said nothing for a moment or so, then a shudder seemed to bring her back to reality.

'It says nothing more than we knew already. It says that he was brave and he fought hard, but an ambush overtook them. They lost many, many men and poor Freddie . . .' She breathed out, a loud puff of air. 'Poor Freddie hurt his leg. He fell and succumbed to some of the gas.' She looked up at me, her eyes bright with tears. 'That gas is evil, Hettie. You heard what your Dad said.'

How could I forget?

I wrapped my arms around Mam's shoulders, nestled my face against her neck. I wouldn't cry. Not now. Mam didn't need that. Her voice sounded chipped and broken; she was not at all like the strong confident Mam I was used to. She never gave into bad thoughts. This wasn't her.

'He's alive,' I whispered. 'He might be a little broken, Mam. He might be suffering. But he's still here when so many aren't.'

Mam swiped her face quickly with her hand. 'That's true. Elsie next door was telling me about Rosie's young boy, Charlie. You remember him?'

I nodded. Of course I did. He lived four doors down from us. He was two years older than Freddie and they'd often knock around together. He was a loud boy, a little overweight, with a hearty laugh that could cut through the street noise like a siren.

'He died, Hettie. They heard just the other day. Killed like a pig in the mud.' She sniffed, her hands trailing across the letter again. 'I know we must be thankful.

I know this. But sometimes I think that your stubborn, good-for-nothing Dad might be right.'

'In what way, Mam?'

'Saying that this is an awful war. It should never have been,' she said firmly. 'So much misery. So much death, and for what, Hettie? Tell me what our boys are dying for? Tell me what this is all for?'

I said nothing, for there was nothing I could say.

There was no answer.

The next day was Saturday. Although it started dark and gloomy, the drizzle soon eased and I offered to hang the sheets out in the yard. The truth was, I needed to get outside. The atmosphere inside the house was oppressive and grim. Dad was still in a dark 'I told you so' kind of mood and had left for work barely speaking to us, and Mam's only concern was to find out whether Freddie had been sent to Moor Park. She had left early to make enquiries. Even though they were both no longer there, I could still feel the sadness and bitterness that had been left behind. I wondered if anything would ever be happy again.

What was our future?

Martha followed me outside clutching a tatty old book.

Her expression was downcast.

'Mam is so cross,' she muttered, kicking at a nearby brick. 'She's shouting at me for everything. I think she must hate me.'

'She doesn't hate you.' I shifted the washing basket on my hip and sighed. 'It's a hard time, that's all. She's worried about Freddie.'

'Is he really coming home?' Martha asked. 'When will he? I want to see him.'

'Soon,' I told her. 'Now hold the end of this sheet and help me fold it, will you.'

The wind caught hold of the sheet and Martha giggled as she jumped up to grip hold of the corner to stop it flying away.

'Will Mam be happy then?' Martha asked quietly. 'When Freddie's back?'

'I hope so,' I said.

'Will Dad?'

I placed the last peg on the sheet and stood back to watch as it lifted in the breeze. It seemed joyful somehow, as if that were even possible. It was free and light.

'I don't know,' I answered honestly.

Martha nodded, she seemed satisfied with the answer. She leant up against the brick wall and lifted her face towards the weak sunlight. She looked so beautiful in that moment, I realised that my little sister was growing up. Her golden hair, so much like Mam's, glittered in the sunlight and her face was thinning out, losing the podginess of childhood.

Out on the street we could hear the rise and fall of shouts and laughter. Martha's eyes immediately lit up and she turned towards the noise.

'The boys are outside. Can we go too?'

I nodded. Why not? I had done all Mam had asked. God knows I needed a break for a minute or two.

We walked through the house and into the street. As soon as we stepped outside the noise swept us up. A few of the lads from Spa Road, Ronnie and Davey Marshall, plus some older boys Will Mercer and Timmy Smith, were kicking around a tin can. Ronnie belted the can across the street, between two discarded jumpers. He already had a decent kick on him. I could imagine Flo, Alice and Grace standing here with me and nodding their approval at his clean strike.

'Goal!' He roared running around in tight little circles, his skinny legs working hard.

Will looked up and seeing us, waved us over. Will was a year or so younger than me, a lovely boy who was not really one to join in with sports. In fact, it was a surprise to see him out today.

'My mam says I need to get outside more,' he said, as if to explain. 'She thinks I'm far too pale.'

I smiled. She had a point. The boy was ghostly white.

'Hey, come and join us, Hettie, we could use the help. We're two-nil down at the moment.'

'I can't, Will,' I said, disappointment gnawing at me. 'I hurt my knee badly.'

I peered down at my leg and remembered my mam's words after her friend visited. The realisation dawned on me all over again. I couldn't even risk a quick kick-around with the boys again without risking further harm. I wanted to cry. Deep, loud tears at the unfairness of it. I'd found something that I actually loved doing and I couldn't do it any more.

'Ey up!'

I spun round. Grace was standing before me, a shy smile cast across her face. It was such a surprise to see her there, totally out of context on my little street, that I actually took a step back and squinted at her. She looked so different in her bright red coat. Her neatly bobbed dark hair was pushed back behind her ears. She looked younger somehow, more unsure.

I don't know if it was because we were out in the daylight, but for the first time I noticed her skin and how it was starting to turn a slight yellowy hue. I wondered why I hadn't seen it before. Perhaps I'd chosen not to?

Was that why Grace had made the comment about the 'canary girls' yesterday? Did she see herself as one now?

'Grace?' I said shyly. 'What a surprise.'

She grinned. 'I was told I'd find you along here somewhere.' She saw my surprise. 'Flo told me.'

'Oh.' I smiled back and then quickly ran my hand across my face, hoping that she hadn't seen the tears that had started to build up.

'I see the boys are having fun,' she said brightly. 'He's a sprightly little one, isn't he?'

'That's Ronnie – he dreams of playing for Preston North End one day.'

'Maybe he will, he's fast enough.' Her smiled faded a little on her lips. 'We need to get through this blessed war though first, don't we?'

'Have you had any more word on your husband?' I asked softly.

'Not really. All I know is that he's in an awful prisoner-of-war camp somewhere. God only knows what he's going through. There is talk that they might free them soon, though.'

'That's good, then?'

'It is, but we don't know who will be released or when it'll happen. It's so very worrying.' She rubbed at her eyes. 'I haven't been sleeping at all recently and I feel sick most days now.' She paused. 'Hettie, I won't be at the factory for a few days. I need to get myself better. I'm going to rest for a little. Try and build up my strength.'

'You're really not well?' I looked at her skin again, but then Grace looked up and caught me staring at her. I quickly averted my gaze, feeling ashamed.

Grace touched her cheek. 'I'm quite the canary now, aren't I?' She giggled. 'I'm half-hoping that yellow will come into fashion, it's not doing much good for my modelling work .'

'You look beautiful,' I said and I really meant it.

Grace's gaze dropped to her feet. 'Thank you, Hettie. You really are too sweet. I wish I could believe you, but . . .' She coughed a little and swiped at her lips. 'I've really not being feeling right for some time. My mam thinks I'm sickening for something. Flo reckons I'm doing too much – I don't know. I've had so much going on recently.'

'You need a rest,' I said gently.

'Yes. Yes I do.'

I glanced at Grace again. In the time that I'd known her, her complexion had changed. Her cheeks were slightly sunken and her eyes had dark circles ringed under them. Quite frankly, she looked as if she was carrying the weight of the world on her shoulders.

'What will you do?' I asked.

'Mam wants me to go to the countryside for a bit,' Grace replied. 'I have an aunt who has a farm out in the middle of nowhere. I can stay there, rest up, help her with her little girl. I like children so I'll not mind that. Hopefully then I'll be better for when Jimmy returns.'

I couldn't imagine Grace not being at the factory. She was such a key part of it.

In fact, she was a key part of everything.

'What of your brother?' Grace asked suddenly. 'Have you heard anything more?'

I nodded. 'Mam is trying to find out about Freddie. She had a letter to say he will be sent home in a few days. She thinks it might be to Moor Park Hospital.'

Moor Park was just across town. It used to be an agricultural pavilion, but now it had been extended into a military hospital for casualties of the war. I think we all hoped Freddie would be sent there. At least it was local.

'It will be all right, you know,' Grace said quietly. 'You have to keep faith.'

I nodded. I couldn't quite find the right words.

For a moment or two we just stood and watched as the boys continued to knock the tired old can along the street. Grace clapped and cheered when a good run or tackle was made.

'You make a great captain,' I said finally.

'Not any more. That honour will go to Alice Kell.'

'Alice?' I said, surprised. I was expecting Grace to chose one of the girls who had already played in the friendly – Alice Standing maybe, or Gertie.

Grace smiled. 'Alice Kell is one of the best footballers I know. I was just waiting for her to find the right time to join us. Now that she has, she will be extraordinary. You just wait. She is a born leader too.'

'I don't doubt it.' I frowned despite myself. 'But Grace, the Dick, Kerr team was started because of you. How can it carry on *without* you?'

'Because a team is more than one player, Hettie.' She turned to me and smiled. 'Don't get me wrong, I love the Dick, Kerr Girls. I want so much to be part of it, but I can't now. Do you understand? I have to do what's right.'

I nodded. Of course I understood. I might not have liked it much. But I did understand.

She sighed. 'I really do think the Dick, Kerr Girls football team will become something amazing. I really believe that.'

'So do I,' I admitted.

And we were no longer part of it. Grace and I. This was our end.

'I'm proud to have been part of it,' Grace said quietly, as if reading my mind. 'Because at the end of the day, it was all I ever wanted – to see our girls do well. I can rest easy if that continues to happen. It'll be such a wonderful thing.'

A sudden feeling of sadness and loss washed over me, I was unable to push it away. She was right, of course. All that mattered was that the girls continued to succeed. This was a much bigger thing than either me or her alone.

'I'll miss it too,' I whispered.

'You can still be part of it. You know that,' she replied firmly. 'The girls still see you as part of the team. They don't want you to push yourself away.'

I bent my head, feeling overwhelmed. 'I don't want to be a burden.'

'You're not a burden, you silly thing,' Grace laughed.

'You're a teammate. You're a Dick, Kerr Girl. So am I, and I always will be.'

A silence passed over us. Grace's words were like a syrup; they soothed and comforted me.

'You're like the big sister I never had,' I said shyly. 'I'm going to miss you so much.'

Grace stroked my arm. 'I'm still with you, Hettie. All the time. You must remember that. Just as I'll be with the girls in every match they play – I'll be with them in spirit, cheering them on. Believing in them. I'll never really be gone.'

I smiled. It was if the pieces of the jigsaw had finally slipped into place.

I might not be able to play any more, but I had still been part of something amazing.

I still could be – but perhaps in another way.

'I wanted to say goodbye,' Grace said. 'But also, thank you.'

Ronnie scored another screamer – and the tin can shot across the street at full speed. He roared with joy.

Inside, I was roaring too.

Mam had finally got confirmation in another letter from Freddie's regiment that he would be sent to Moor Park hospital in the next few days. There still wasn't much detail contained in the letter, only that Freddie had been 'brave throughout battle' and that gas and a bullet to the leg had overcome him. As Mam had said softly, he was probably lucky to make it out of there at all.

I'd nodded, feeling a little better. But still an uneasiness gnawed at my stomach.

I just wanted to see Freddie for myself, to know that he was really going to be all right. It was the not knowing that was killing me. The bad thoughts and worries were taking over my mind. I needed to see his face, to take his hand in mine and know for sure that he was home for good.

Flo met me at the end of the road before work. She was alone this time and her usually trouble-free face looked sad as I approached. She walked towards me and smiled, but I could see that it didn't quite reach her eyes. I knew immediately what was wrong.

'You saw Grace, didn't you?'

Flo nodded. She wiped her nose and sniffed. 'I know it's daft, but I hate the thought of her being gone.'

'She told me she'd only be away for a short while,' I replied, frowning.

'Aye, I know,' Flo shrugged. 'And perhaps she will. But she was ill before, last winter. She had an infection that got right into her chest – it made her so poorly. I'm not sure a short while will be enough. You know how hard the factory work is.'

That I did know. I didn't tell Flo, but I was only too relieved to be working with Mr Frankland now. It was far more pleasant to be in the quiet office away from the loud machines, not to mention the awful chemicals and constant fear of explosions. Just thinking of all that again made me remember Grace's yellow skin and tired eyes – she really hadn't looked right. I glanced up at Flo, but luckily there didn't seem to be a trace of that awful colour on her.

'Don't you worry about it?' I asked. 'Becoming a canary?'

Flo giggled lightly. 'Oh, I reckon we've got more to worry about than a bit of colouring. Anyway, one of the girls says it's only temporary. It soon lifts once you're away from the munitions for a bit. I'd rather not worry if I don't have to.'

I smiled shyly. If only I could be more like that . . . I admired Flo's bright and positive outlook to life. Nothing seemed to worry her.

We started walking. I was still going at a much slower pace due to my inflamed knee. I couldn't put full weight on it, but Flo didn't seem to mind. She kept right beside me, like my guardian, and took my arm to help me over the more tricky steps or cobbles.

'I'll miss Grace at the factory,' Flo said as we walked. 'She was always such a laugh, so keen to keep busy. And look what she started with the football! Now the girls can't stop talking about it. Alice has been putting the word about – trying to drum up some interest.'

I paused. 'Grace said that she thinks Alice should be the captain now.'

Flo nodded. 'I couldn't think of anyone more suited to the job. Alice is a better defender than any boy I've ever met – my goodness, that girl grew up surrounded by the sport, her whole family are into it. She would do a wonderful job of it.'

'What do you think of Mr Frankland helping out?' I asked.

Flo smiled. 'Oh yes. I think that's really exciting, actually. We have someone who believes in the team. Someone who wants to help us. What could be better than that?' She glanced over and I saw her eyes fall on my knee. 'Maybe . . . once your knee is better . . . you can join us again. You're certainly handy on the wing.'

'I don't know,' I said. 'But I'm sure you'll find other fast girls. Alice told me about one – Lily – she sounds fantastic.'

Flo was almost bouncing along the street in glee. 'I know. It's so exciting. I've been told of at least two girls that could be good upfront and perhaps another winger.'

'You just need some matches,' I mused. 'Mr Frankland was talking of arranging games with other women's teams. Apparently, there are a few dotted around.'

'Yes, there are. All over Lancashire. That would be good,' Flo agreed. 'If not, we can play – the boys again. As long as they play by the rules this time.'

'And you'll still be involved,' Flo said firmly to me. 'If you can't play, you can't play – but we'll not have you excluded. You're part of the journey. Even if you're handing out half-time oranges, we all want you there.'

'Thanks,' I said, smiling shyly. 'Let's just wait and see, eh?'

I suppose handing out oranges was better than nothing, but still my stomach twisted at the thought of not being able to play.

Flo paused and grabbed my shoulders, turning me to look at her. Her eyes were blazing with passion as she stared down at me with such intensity it almost made me flinch.

'Don't you see, Hettie – once you're part of the Dick, Kerr Girls, you always will be. It'll be in your heart for ever.' She paused, licked her lips. 'And in the same way, every woman who plays for the team will be part of its history, part of something amazing and special. No one can take that away from you.'

I stared up at her. I wasn't sure what to say in reply, no words seemed appropriate, but something was stirring inside of me. It was that same feeling of hope that had come from Grace before.

'I'm right, aren't I, Hettie,' she said. It was a statement. Not a question.

I nodded.

At least, I very much hoped that she was.

It was busy in the office with Mr Frankland, who seemed to be in an upbeat mood – especially when I told him how excited the girls were.

'I think they like the idea of you managing them,' I said. 'Anything to help the football team get off the ground properly.'

'Excellent news.' Mr Frankland considered it, his hands clasped in front of him. 'There are so many plans to be made. We need to organise kit – although for the time being, they will have to continue to wear the boys' second kit. In time they will need their own . . . And we need a ground, of course. I must make some enquiries . . .'

'And teams to play,' I added.

He glanced up, looking for a moment as if he'd forgotten I was there. 'Oh yes, indeed. Teams. Other ladies' teams. There are ones I know of. I will make contact, make some arrangements . . .' He slapped his hands in excitement. 'Oh, Hettie, I really think I can start to make things happen! Before long, everyone will know who the Dick, Kerr Girls are.'

I smiled back. 'I never doubted it, Mr Frankland.'

Later, in the dinner hall, I relayed the news to Alice, Flo and Gertie.

'So, with any luck, you should have some teams set up to play soon,' I said eagerly. 'How about that?'

Alice reached over and squeezed my hand. 'I think

it's wonderful. I think Mr Frankland really can give us the best start possible. Thank you so much for making it happen, Hettie.'

'Alice is already arranging trials for this weekend,' Flo said. 'Isn't that exciting! We've had so much interest. Even young George wanted to sign up.'

'I'm not sure he meets the criteria of being a lady,' Gertie said dryly. 'Or the criteria for being a decent player.'

I smiled. I couldn't think too many vengeful thoughts towards George. The poor lad had been avoiding me since my injury. I knew he felt awful about it now.

'Either way – some of the lads think we could be the best team in the area.' Alice's face was glowing. 'Fancy that, the boys actually thinking that we might be any good.'

'Well, they've seen us play,' replied Flo. 'Who can blame them?'

The boys had certainly seen the likes of Florrie Rance, who was fast and strong up-front and never gave up. And Alice Standing, a battling midfielder with a clear head and a strong tackle. And Gertie, with her two quick feet and sharp decisions.

But they still hadn't properly seen the likes of Alice Kell, who was a strong and robust defender, or Flo, who was a very sharp shooter, or this young girl, Lily Jones – who, as much as I hated to say it, sounded like she could be a much better winger than me. What a team this could be.

'What's up with you, Hettie? Dreaming again?' Gertie teased.

I smiled. 'I am a bit. It's all so exciting for you.'

'It is,' Alice replied. 'But we need to get serious too. I want girls who can play well but who work hard as a team. This is our family now – you have to earn your place.'

Flo nodded. 'Too right. There'll be lots out there who'll want us to do badly so that they can make a big show of saying, "I told you so".'

I thought of my dad and frowned. I knew how much he'd like to see the girls fail.

'That's why we have to pick carefully,' Alice said firmly. 'We will train harder and faster than any boy. We'll be more determined and more keen to win. We might have to prove our ability – but so be it. We will make everyone see that women can play football too. This isn't only a boys' sport. It's our sport too.'

'And we can be good at it,' Flo added. 'Great, in fact.'

'All this is worthless, though, unless we can arrange a proper match against a proper team,' Alice said. 'And who knows when that'll be . . .'

But the answer came sooner than we thought.

A full week passed before we got the news we were waiting for – Freddie was at Moor Park. I don't know if it was the nerves or relief, but I immediately felt a rush of sickness at the news. Could I face seeing him? Would he still look the same? Would he still be our Freddie?

Mam told me the news as I soon as I'd returned from my Thursday shift at work. She was planning to go and see him the next day and wondered if I could go too, after my shift.

'He'll want to see us,' she said. Her gaze flicked towards Dad, who was home early again and reading a newspaper in the corner of the room. He didn't respond.

'Of course I'll go,' I replied.

'He'll love to hear your news, about the goings-on at the factory and that little football match you took part in.'

My skin immediately prickled. 'It wasn't a *little* match, Mam. We took on the boys and won.'

'Of course you did,' Mam said, but she was distracted, a ghost of a smile painted on her face. I could see her thoughts were elsewhere, already thinking of her beloved son and what she would say when she saw him.

'You won't be talking to him about any such nonsense,' Dad muttered from the corner. He put down his paper and stared at both of us. 'The sooner this house goes back to normal, the better. I want no more talk of football.'

'Why not?' Mam's voice was like ice – I'd never heard it like that before.

'The poor boy has been through quite enough. He doesn't need to hear Hettie's silly stories and daft ideas.' His gaze was now fixed on mine and he slowly shook his head. 'The boy has been to hell and back. He won't want to be told about some daft, deluded women who think that they can actually play a man's sport. And for what? What good does it do?'

'For pleasure,' I whispered.

'Pleasure?' Dad repeated quietly. He sounded almost regretful. 'Pleasure? Hettie, do you really think we can be allowed such a thing at times like this? Do you think that's something we are entitled to?'

'But, Dad—'

'There's no "buts" about it. His voice overshadowed mine. 'Pleasure is irrelevant now. The only important thing is survival. One day, Hettie, you might come to understand that. All talk of football is banned.' He glared at me. 'And I hope, I sincerely hope, that you have stopped hanging around with these women. Honestly, the men in the pub are already blathering on about it. Word is getting around that these silly lasses think they are the next best thing. If they got wind that my daughter was involved, I'd never hear the end of it.'

I stared back, shocked. I wasn't aware that gossip had already started in the pubs. Was this the impact the Dick, Kerr Girls were already making?

'Tell me you'll not be involved with them any more,' he barked.

I bowed my head, not wanting to lie to my father. 'I see them at work, Dad. They are my friends.'

'Well you need to stop circulating with the wrong types of people, Hettie. I mean it, young lady. If I catch any wind that you are getting involved with that group again – I'll have your guts for garters. Do you hear me? I'll not have it.'

I nodded slowly. 'I hear you.'

How could I not hear him? His words were like bullets, tearing through me. I only wished I hadn't heard him. I only wished I could block him out.

How could I turn my back on the only friends I had?

But, at the same time, how could I disobey my own father?

I couldn't win.

Later that evening, I slipped away into the kitchen. I was sitting quietly, drinking my cocoa and trying desperately to stop my thoughts from tumbling down a dark path.

'Penny for them?'

I looked up. Dad stood in the doorway. He'd left to go to the pub a few hours before but was back home earlier than usual. I could tell from his steady stance that he hadn't had 'one too many' this time.

'I was thinking of Freddie,' I said quietly. 'And the war.'

'Ah.' Dad stood rooted to the spot as if considering this for a moment, then he stepped forward. 'You must think of me as unkind most days.'

'No,' I said, even though this was a lie, for most days he *was* unkind.

'I–I have views that are different from many.' Dad snorted and then carefully moved around towards the table and eased himself into the chair opposite mine. I heard the soft groan as he sat down, saw his eyes narrow with pain. 'You see, many men – women too – think that this war, this Great War, is a good thing. But I hate it. I hate everything it stands for.'

'Dad, you mustn't say that,' I urged. 'You could get into awful trouble.'

Dad flapped his hand at me. 'What does it matter? I'm too old to fight, anyway. I'll be working my backside off down at the docks until the day I drop. That's how it is. I work. I get paid a pittance and then for a few hours I escape to sit with loud men as they shout off their opinions and moan about their lot. You talked about pleasure earlier, Hettie . . . I used to think that was my pleasure, but now, I wonder . . .'

'Aren't you happy, Dad?' I asked softly.

The ache inside me had grown. I'd always known Dad was in pain. We all saw the darkness that overshadowed him, but I'd never really considered that he might be desperately sad, too.

'This is my life,' Dad muttered. 'I make do. I try my best.'

I thought of the hours he worked, tirelessly, despite his pain. How much that must wear him down. 'I know you do,' I replied.

'My children – that's what matters. Freddie, you, Martha. The thought of my boy injured in a war that he shouldn't have been involved in breaks my heart. He's only a lad, Hettie. He's sixteen, far too young—'

His voice broke. His head dipped and shoulders slumped. I reached across and gripped his hand. The skin was so tough and gnarly it reminded me of the bark on a tree.

'Dad . . .'

He looked up. His dark eyes fixed on mine. His mouth opened, and for a moment I thought he was going to say something more. But then, quite suddenly, he shrugged off my grip and turned away from me.

'Go now, Hettie, please. I want to be alone.'

'But, Dad–'

'Just go!'

At work the next day, all attention seemed to be on the Dick, Kerr Girls and their ambitious plans. The trial was now the talk of the shop floor. I'd even heard a couple of girls giggling about it on the way into work, reckoning they could give it a shot. There was a sudden burst of energy among the women that something exciting could be happening.

'I want a part of this,' one woman had whispered to her friend in the queue for lunch. 'It beats staying indoors all day helping with the chores.'

'Me too,' her friend had said. 'My mam keeps saying

I'm too strong for my own good. Now's my chance to put it to good use.'

I'd listened to the chatter with a wry smile. Of course, jealousy still nibbled away inside of me and thoughts of what Dad had said last night still troubled me. But also, a bubble of pride was swelling inside too. This was something us girls had created, but it was thanks to Grace's hard work. It was all because of her we had the team.

I only wished she was here now to see the effect it was having on the women in the factory.

It was hard to concentrate in Mr Frankland's office too, even though I had plenty of filing to do. The other apprentices kept asking me questions and one of the lads, a skinny, spiteful-looking boy named Roger, dared to ask why the girls were even bothering.

'They'll only show themselves up,' he said scornfully. 'Women playing football. It's not right, is it?'

Tim, who sat beside him, sniggered a little but then, seeing my angry expression, quickly covered his mouth. 'I'm sure the women will put in a good effort,' he mumbled behind his hand.

Roger snorted. 'It's not right. All this women's rights nonsense. When will it end?' His eyes drilled into mine, like I could supply all of the answers. I think he was a year or so older than me although he didn't look it, on account of his scrawny frame. 'It was the flippin' suffragettes that started it all. My dad says the men talk about them all night at the pub – say they're ruining this country.'

I immediately thought of Dad and what he had said the night before. He must've heard similar conversations. Perhaps he'd joined in? Laughed along with them.

'Just be glad Mr Frankland isn't able to hear you,' I said curtly. 'He believes in the women, even if you lot don't.'

As if on cue, Mr Frankland strode into the office, carrying what looked like another pile of filing in his arms. As usual he was wearing a bright smile, which seemed to light up the room as he walked in.

'What was that?' he barked merrily, placing the pile of papers on my desk. 'Did I hear someone say my name?'

'It was nothing, sir,' Roger replied sharply, flashing me a warning look. 'We were just larking around, weren't we, Hettie?'

'Were we?' I stared him down and then quickly turned my attention back to my boss. 'Oh, I suppose we were, Mr Frankland. In fact, Roger here was telling me how much he respects and admires the very idea of a Dick, Kerr girls' team.'

Tim spluttered into his hand and quickly turned away.

Seemingly unbothered, Mr Frankland rocked back on his heels and addressed Roger cheerily. 'Oh, that is good to know, Mr Neville. We need young men like you out there, supporting our ladies.'

'Of course I will,' Roger said, straight-faced, his eyes only momentarily flicking towards me. 'It would be an honour.'

'An honour?' Mr Frankland repeated the word, as if testing it. 'Now that is grand. Perhaps you and some of your friends could come to the ladies' first match. Show some support? It would be very much appreciated.'

Roger bowed his head a little, shot a quick look at Tim. 'Oh yes, I'll be there,' he replied. 'I'm sure Tim will come as well, won't you?'

Tim looked up nervously. 'Ah – ah, yes – of course.'

'Fantastic!' Mr Frankland clapped his hands together. 'It's imperative that we drum up support and interest. Before long, the whole of Preston will talking about the Dick, Kerr Girls.'

'Oh, I'm sure they will, sir,' Roger said smoothly. But the way he said it suggested that he believed they would be talked about for all the wrong reasons. I flashed him a cool glare, but he simply grinned in response.

What an idiot!

'Now – you seem a little sad today, Hettie,' Mr Frankland said matter-of-factly, turning his attention to me. 'If you don't mind me saying, you look rather pale too. Is your knee bothering you still?'

I glanced down at my leg. I'd not given it much thought, but if I were to move too fast or stand for too long it began to throb. I wasn't sure that Mam's hot compresses were making much of a difference, even though she swore by them.

'It's such a shame,' Mr Frankland continued. 'I was hoping that you might be able to attend the trial on Saturday.'

My cheeks reddened; I immediately thought of Dad and what I had promised.

'I can't play, sir,' I stuttered. 'I don't know what use I'll be.'

Mr Frankland leant forward a little, his voice softening. 'Alice just asked me to ask you. She'd really like you there, even if it's just for a short while. Another pair of eyes, I reckon. A bit of moral support?'

I smiled. I did very much want to watch the trial, to see how the other girls looked.

'It would mean a lot . . .' he continued. 'She also said Grace would want you there.'

I swallowed. Grace. I thought of her smiling, kind face and how much I missed her. Saturday morning,

Dad would be at work. He didn't need to know that I would be at the trial. And it would only be a one-off. I owed Grace that much, at least.

'All right,' I said quietly. 'I'll come for a little bit.'

'Wonderful,' he replied keenly. 'I'm hearing that turnout will be good, so we need to ensure that we pick the fittest and most able girls.'

'That sounds like a good plan.'

'I've already arranged for us to use the men's old kit,' he continued brightly. 'It's not much, I'm afraid, but it should do us a turn.'

And will be far too big, I thought privately. But never mind, it was something at least.

'I should have more news about a ground soon, too.' He bent forward and whispered quickly. 'I'm in talks with another team. If it pays off, the girls will have somewhere to play.'

'That's great news.'

'It is indeed.' He righted himself and looked down at me, concern still etched on his face. 'Are you sure you're all right, Hettie? You do seem a little off colour.'

I wanted to tell him about Freddie – how terribly nervous I was about my planned visit to the hospital. But Mr Frankland seemed so cheerful, so positive, that I really didn't want to darken his mood.

'I'm quite all right,' I said, flashing him my brightest smile. 'In fact, I couldn't be better.'

I felt a million times worse by the evening. On the tram journey to the hospital, I sat with my nose pressed up against the window watching numbly as the streets of Preston glided past me. I had to catch two trams – one into town and one out to Moor Park – but I didn't mind. I quite liked the time to myself. Signs of the war were everywhere and many shops were already closed because of the lack of trade. It was as if Preston itself was hanging on by a thread. A ghost town of what it once was.

I thought of Freddie that last time I had seen him, standing out among the crowd of men. How he had turned to us and waved, his dark hair whipping back in the wind and his cheeks rosy from the cold. He had looked so healthy, strong and confident – not scared at all. How I wished I had run through the crowd. I wish I had grabbed him by the collar of his stiff uniform and tugged him away from the others.

He never should have gone. Not my Freddie.

He wasn't ready.

The tram pulled up to a stop and I hopped off and

trundled up the road to Moor Park. The evening air had quite a kick to it and I had to bend my head against the sharp breeze that rushed through my hair as I half-ran towards the building.

I looked up to take in the sight. In front of me stood a series of pre-fabricated huts. On the drive outside was a large flagpole and the Union Jack fluttered defiantly in greeting. I saw a man dressed in khaki sitting in a wheelchair by the entrance. He was sucking on a cigarette and scowling into the distance.

'Good evening,' I said cheerfully in greeting.

His eyes turned to mine. They had a glassy expression. 'Is it?' he replied, and then he looked away again.

I quickly entered the main building through a low porched door with a cross marked above it. I was soon caught up in the medley of noise and smells that hit me. It was much brighter than the factory and the sounds were so different – loud voices dominated the space. And cries and moans. I couldn't shut out those sounds, no matter how hard I tried; they seemed to be coming from every direction. The stink of disinfectant was burning my nostrils.

I saw two nurses huddled together beside a small table and approached them cautiously.

'Hello. I wonder if perhaps you could help?' I said quickly.

They both looked up. One, an older woman, frowned slightly and cocked her head slightly in my direction. 'Yes?'

'It's my brother – Freddie Blakeford. I believe he has been brought here.'

'I don't know—' the older nurse began, but then the second nurse touched her hand.

'Mavis – I think she means the young boy, brought in yesterday?'

'Ah, yes,' Nurse Mavis nodded. Her expression completely softened. 'Forgive me, it's been a long day. As you will see, we have rather a lot of men brought here.' She smiled gently and beckoned me in her direction. 'Follow me. I'll take you to him now.'

She swept me through a door and into one of the low-rise buildings. Immediately my eyes were drawn to the many beds lined up along each side. I tried not to look as we passed by but it was so hard not to, especially as the men were crying out as we passed.

'Oh – please. Please help me.'

'I can't. I can't . . .'

'No more . . . no more!'

The men all seemed to be in different states of distress. Some were sat up in bed, bandages covering their injuries. Some had their legs up in a cast. Others were laying static, completely still under the covers.

Mavis cast a cautious eye in my direction. 'The loud ones aren't even the worst,' she confided. 'It's the quiet ones that get to you. The ones that lie there and don't say a word, their entire body a quivering mess. You wonder what's going on inside of them. What they're thinking about.'

'It's – it's so awful,' I gasped.

As we reached the end of the room, my eyes fell on a man laid flat on his back. His face was completely bandaged, and he looked as though he might be sleeping.

'Mustard gas,' Mavis whispered. 'Evil. Burns everything. Skin, lungs. Everything.' She paused. 'We can't even find family for him. How bad is that?'

I wanted to stop. I wanted to stand by this poor man for a while. Find out his name, discover who he was. I hated to think of him lying here all alone, so badly injured – but Mavis was already urging me on.

'It's getting late. You won't have long with him,' she said. 'He'll need his sleep.'

It was only then that I realised that Mavis was

standing by the foot of the last bed, the one right beside the bandaged man.

Fear clawed at my belly as I walked towards her towards this last bed.

The covers were drawn up tight and a pale face rested against the pillow. A face so pale and thin that I barely recognised it. Dark, mournful eyes that looked as though they had been hollowed out of his skull, stared up bleakly at the ceiling. Reedy, white hands clasped the edges of the blanket as if they were frightened to let go.

As I stepped nearer I could hear the rattle of his breathing, like there were tiny pebbles in his chest.

'Freddie!' I whispered. 'Oh, Freddie.'

And then, even though I really didn't want to, I burst into tears.

'Freddie.' I gripped one of his thin hands in mine. 'You poor, poor thing.'

How could a person change so much in so little time? I counted back the months. He'd left us just before the summer and now it was November – and yet, the person before me barely looked like my brother. I wondered how it was possible for someone to change so much.

That was until he eased himself up in the bed slightly, tipped his head towards mine and flashed me a wide smile. His dimples still stood out in his grey cheeks. His eyes still shone with a light merriment that I remembered from before. If I ignored the sunken state of his eyes and the wheeze in his chest, I could almost convince myself that he was still quite all right. It was the same boy I remembered.

'Do I really look that awful, Hettie? My goodness, looking at your face I'm beginning to imagine the worst.'

'You don't look awful,' I said. 'Just . . .'

What? Tired? Older? Greyer? It was difficult to

describe but despite his best efforts to grin, it felt like some of Freddie's energy and warmth had drained away.

'What happened?' I asked instead.

'Well . . .' he replied slowly. 'I was shot at. That's what happened. The enemy caught us with the gas. It totally took over everything. I couldn't make anything out. I couldn't breathe and then as I fell, they caught me in my leg—'

He shook his head; I noticed his grip on the blanket had tightened.

'I don't remember getting shot if I'm honest. I just fell. One of the lads saw me and dragged me into a dugout. They got me right here, in the thigh. Want to see?'

I shook my head. 'No thanks.'

'It'll scar nicely.' He coughed and I heard the deep rattle again. 'I expect that'll be my footballing career over.'

I flinched instinctively at his words. He might not be alone there. What would he think if I told him so . . .?

Mavis was busying herself at the end of the bed, straightening the sheets and checking Freddie's notes, but she looked up at Freddie's words.

'Now, now Freddie – no focusing on the negative. You heard what the doctor said.'

Freddie sighed. 'Yes, that I need to keep my pecker up. Not so easy when you're laid out in here though.'

He paused, bit his lip a little – something he always did when he was agitated. 'They say I'll always walk with a limp. There's far too much damage to the muscle, apparently. And my lungs . . .' He gestured wildly at his chest. 'Who knows how bad they are. Once that gas gets hold, it's a guessing game really.'

'You will get better,' I said firmly. 'You promised me. Remember?'

'Aye, I said the same to Mam this morning.' Freddie laughed. 'You know, I've never seen the woman look so upset. I swear she almost cried in front of me.'

I sucked in a breath. We both knew how unlike Mam that was. She'd normally rather die than show any form of emotion. It was seen as weakness in her eyes.

'She has been upset,' I told him. 'So worried. Dad too.'

Freddie laughed louder, which resulted in another burst of uncontrollable coughing. 'Now you are having me on. Dad? Upset over me? Never!'

'He really was,' I insisted. 'After all, he never wanted you to go in the first place.'

'That's true.' Freddie bowed his head. 'It could have been worse, though. Look at Micky Adams in the next bed, the same gas caught him full in the face. He didn't have his mask on . . .'

'You came in together?' I paused. 'I'm so sorry.'

'Don't be sorry. It's war. It's a dirty business,' he said, his tone lowering to barely a whisper. 'Micky is as tough as boots. He'll get through it, I'm sure . . .'

His voice drifted and I noticed that his gaze did too. I squeezed his hand again.

'I'm sure he will be just fine.'

'Aye – well, never mind all this. I can't stand to lie around in bed all day listening to the sound of my own voice. It gets tiring. Tell me about you. Tell me what you've been up to. Mam tells me you're working at Dick, Kerr's now.'

I sat up straighter, all of a sudden feeling brighter. 'I am! And would you believe that I'm now working with Mr Frankland – I mean, I wasn't to start with. I was on the shop floor with the other girls, stuffing the munitions – by God that was a tough job – but when I hurt my knee, Mr Frankland said I could work with him.'

Freddie chuckled softly. 'I see you've not lost the gift of the gab!' His soft eyes scanned mine. 'You hurt your knee? How? Were they working you too hard?'

'No, it wasn't that. I hurt it playing football.'

Freddie laughed a little louder. 'Football! Are you pulling my leg, Hettie? Because that would be cruel, on account of my injury.'

I smiled shyly. 'I'm not pulling your leg, Fred. I was playing football. For a while. The girls have set up a team and . . .' I pulled myself closer to him, feeling a little self-conscious. 'And they're rather bloody good, I have to say. I'm only upset that I can't play any more. We took on the lads at the factory and actually beat them. Many say we totally outplayed them.'

Freddie shook his head slowly. 'Well I never! I'm away for a few months and look what happens – my little sister turns into a footballer. I have to say, I never expected that.'

I lowered my gaze. 'I'm hardly a footballer, Freddie. Not now, anyway. My knee is knackered. It hurts every time I move it. And Dad . . .'

Freddie's face hardened a little. 'Dad, what?'

'Dad doesn't want me to play. He says that it's not what women like me should be doing,' I sniffed. 'I think he thinks I deserved the injury.'

Freddie shook his head. 'How familiar this all sounds. Remember how Dad didn't want me to go to war, too? How he said it wasn't right for me to be out there fighting?' He paused, a short sharp cough biting through his words. He swiped at his mouth and continued. 'I wonder whether he thinks the same of me – that I deserved to get injured? That this is my punishment?'

'I . . . no . . . I'm sure–'

'Do you regret playing, Hettie?' Freddie shot back. 'Do you regret getting involved?'

'Not all at,' I replied firmly. 'I really enjoyed it. For once, it felt like I was doing something . . .' I felt flustered, unable to find the right words.

'Something good?' Freddie offered. 'You were helping others? You were part of a team? You see – that was the same for me, Hettie. That's why I don't regret this injury at all. I'm sad, obviously. I'm a bit fed up. But I don't regret it. While I was out there, I was among some of the bravest and funniest lads I've ever met. We kept each other going. We were a family.'

I thought of the Dick, Kerr Girls, and of Grace, Alice and Flo especially, and found myself nodding along. We were a family too. I was part of something good.

'So you don't think it's wrong for me to be involved with the team?' I asked.

'Not at all. In fact, I think it's a bloody good thing to do. As it happens, I always thought you had a decent touch on you. But what a shame you've done your knee in. The same thing happened to my mate, Harry Towns. He was never the same after. It can be an awful injury.'

'It doesn't matter, anyway,' I replied. 'The important

thing is the girls have a team now. Mr Frankland is going to help manage them and arrange some games. They hope it will be good for the community to see the team coming together and doing well.'

'I only hope others think the same,' Freddie said gently. 'There will be many, your traditional types like Dad, who won't want to see women on a football pitch. They will object at every opportunity. The girls need to prepare themselves for that.'

I sighed. 'I suppose we hope to change those opinions.'

Freddie squeezed my hand tightly in his. 'I reckon you might be able to,' he said firmly. 'And I for one would like to see it happen. I'll be cheering you on all the way.'

Mavis showed me out. We walked back the same way we came and this time I tried not to avert my eyes as we passed the many beds that were lined up along our path. These men were other peoples' brothers, sons. Sweethearts. Once again, my thoughts turned to Grace and I wondered if she had heard from her Jimmy. Could he be lying in a bed like this somewhere, waiting for her? Who could blame her for wanting to step away from everything at Dick, Kerr, when she had so much going on?

I found myself looking over at a bed in the far corner

where a man lay sleeping. It was clear from the lumps under the sheets that his legs stopped after his knees.

'It makes you realise, doesn't it...' Mavis said suddenly, noticing where my eyes had fallen. 'The true cost of war.'

'It really does,' I replied quietly, the words catching in my throat.

'Aye,' Mavis agreed. 'And of course, we can only treat the injuries we see. For many, the true pain runs far, far deeper.'

We swept through into the main entrance hall. Mavis turned to me, touching my arm lightly.

'I'm just glad you could come. It's so important that patients like Freddie have their families around them.'

'But he will be all right, won't he?' My voice was wavering. 'I mean – it's just a leg injury and some gas to his lungs. He will recover?'

Mavis's deep-set eyes held my gaze. 'I'm hoping Freddie's leg will heal just fine, his lungs too, but he sure as heck won't be running any races from now on. Like I said before, some wounds run deeper. We can only wait to see how long it takes for them to heal.'

'I suppose you're right,' I said, feeling unsure as to what exactly she meant. Surely once Freddie healed and came home, he would be back to his old self again. He needed to get back into his old routine again, that was all.

'Hello. I don't think we've seen you here before, now have we?'

I turned round. Standing behind me was a very tall, stern-looking woman with grey hair swept into a tight bun. At first I thought her expression was quite hostile, but then she broke into a smile and her entire face lit up with warmth. I immediately relaxed.

'Indeed, Matron,' Mavis said politely. 'This is Hettie. She came to visit our new lad, young Freddie, straight after her shift at the Dick, Kerr factory. I imagine she's had a long day.'

'That is dedication, indeed,' Matron said. She reached out and shook my hand, her grip was strong and warm. 'And you really work at Dick, Kerr's, do you?'

'Yes . . . yes, I do.'

'So many young women working there now. It's good to see,' she replied stoutly. 'About time this damn country made more use of our resources, eh?'

'Indeed.' I grinned back at her.

'In fact, it's quite a coincidence I should run into you today,' she continued brightly. 'I was hoping to speak to someone over at that factory about an idea I have.'

Curiosity prickled me. 'Oh – what was that?'

'Well . . .' She paused, folded her arms across her body

and leant towards me. 'As you are probably aware, this entire hospital relies on charitable donations. You could say that we are struggling somewhat, what with the sheer number of patients that have been sent to us. Of course, we will cope, we always do, but some more funding would really help the cause.'

I nodded, understanding immediately, my mind moving once again to the many men I had passed in their beds. So many needed help and who knew how many more would come through these doors? Before long, the entire hospital would become overcrowded. I wasn't quite sure how they would manage then.

'Is there anything I can do to help?' I asked. 'I mean – I might not be very powerful, but I may be able to speak to someone at the factory?'

'I was thinking of a fundraising event,' Matron said keenly. 'I know Dick, Kerr have helped with such things before. Perhaps a fair, or a dance, or a—'

'A football match?' I finished for her.

'Well, er, yes? Maybe.' Matron seemed uncertain. 'If you think you can get the numbers? You'd need a decent side for people to be interested. Good players must be thin on the ground right now with all the men being called up.'

'Not the ones I'm thinking of,' I replied.

'I'm not sure I understand . . .'

'Matron, how would you feel if we were to organise a charity football match between two good teams. Two women's teams.' I watched as her eyes widened a little. My confidence grew. I couldn't help myself. 'After all, it is time that this damn country made more use of our resources, eh?'

A bright smile spread across Matron's thin white face. 'Indeed it is,' she said softly. 'Indeed it is.'

'I still can't believe we have a team who want to play us!' Alice said excitedly. 'And Arundel Coulthard, too! I've heard they are a pretty decent side.'

Arundel Coulthard Foundry were a neighbouring team also based on Marsh Lane. Mr Frankland had been delighted when he had manged to secure their agreement to play against us in the charity match. Apparently word had got to some of their girls about our game with the boys, and they were keen to face us.

'We have something to work towards now, Hettie,' Mr Frankland said proudly.

All the Dick, Kerr Girls needed now was a confirmed, stable team.

We were back at the same park where we had played the boys, ready to start the trials. Across the field a group of women were gathered, busy warming up while wearing an assortment of oversized kit – most of it likely borrowed from relatives or lads that they knew in the street. They really did look like a mismatched crew.

I was standing alongside Alice Kell, Florrie Rance, Alice Standing and Flo – who were helping to oversee the warm-up. I guessed they were all shoo-ins for the team. Now we needed to complete the strong set-up.

Of course, I wasn't really meant to be here. If Dad got wind of it, he would tan my hide. But I had promised Alice I would come and decided that a few hours would be all right. After all, it wasn't as if I was directly involved with the team. I was only watching them.

'If we play well against Coulthard, who knows where it will lead?' Florrie said, her eyes glowing. 'Not to mention the money we could raise for the hospital. God knows they need it.'

'I just hope that we can get lots of spectators,' I said, thinking of the matron at the hospital. 'Will people really pay to watch women play? You know what they can be like.'

'Even a few spectators would be good, Hettie,' Flo said brightly. 'We have to be grateful for any interest, don't we?'

'Grace will be so proud of us raising money for the hospital. It was always so important to her that the soldiers were well cared for,' Alice said quietly. 'I only wish she could be here today. It seems wrong somehow, not to have her with us.'

'At the match, we will play in her honour,' Flo said

defiantly. 'The game will be for Grace.'

I watched as Mr Frankland strolled along the park to join us. He was still dressed formally in his suit and tie, but his usually immaculate hair was being whipped up by the steady breeze. He reached up to try and tame it.

'Bracing day!' he barked. 'But at least the rain has held off.'

'The surface should be good enough to put the girls through their paces,' Alice Kell agreed. 'We need to see who can run with the ball. Who can make and receive firm passes. Who is able to stand up well to the tackle.'

Mr Frankland nodded. 'With any luck, we should be able to select a decent side from this lot. I have to say, I'm delighted at the numbers. It seems women really do want to play football.'

Alice simply grinned at him. 'You never needed to doubt that.'

Alice worked the girls hard. In fact, for once I was glad of my injury, as I could enjoy watching from the sidelines as she barked out instructions and demonstrated tricks and skills that she had learnt from her brothers.

'Alice Kell is a born leader,' Mr Frankland said, with admiration. 'She will make an amazing captain.'

'She certainly knows how to motivate the other girls,' I agreed.

We watched as the women ran from one side of the field to the other, as they performed various exercises usually reserved for an army personal training class. The trial ended with a number of five-a-side games.

'The benefit of having an older brother who's a footballer,' Alice had confessed to us earlier, 'is that I can steal so many of his drills and exercises.'

The drills also gave us an opportunity to work out which girls showed real promise. Certainly a small group of women stood out early on.

Gertie played particularly well in the mini games, showing flashes of brilliance in front of goal and a strength and confidence that had seemed to increase since her game against the boys. Alice put her on the list almost immediately.

'Gertie Whittle has to play,' she said firmly. 'The girl is a born fighter.'

Other stand-out players included Evie Clayton, Lily Jones and Elise Nixon, who went on Alice's list quite swiftly. Not only were these girls able to show their quick feet in training, they were also able to demonstrate their strength and determination in the games. Likewise,

Flo Redford showed why she had a great reputation – moving with great pace throughout the session and scoring some wonderful goals.

It wasn't long before the trial ended and the group stood before Alice, all red-faced and puffy, hands resting on knees and sweat dribbling down their faces. It was quite a sight! Never before had I seen such a worn-out pack of women. Nor such a happy and contented lot!

Alice conferred with Mr Frankland for a moment a little way behind me on the sidelines. Then the women came towards me, taking turns to congratulate each other.

'It'll be so good to be a part of this,' one said loudly. 'If not only to shut up my fat slob of a husband. He only thinks us women are good enough for cooking and rearing babies.'

'Mine's the same. His head nearly exploded when I told him where I was going today,' another stated, her hands planted stoutly on her hips. 'Off to play football? Whatever next, woman? You'll be wanting to vote and party next.'

'Chance would be a fine thing,' the first added, and the group exploded with laughter.

''Ere, aren't you one of the girls that played the first game?' said the second woman, peering at me. 'Is it true what they say? That you can't play any more?'

I nodded, sadness clawing at me once again. 'I've clobbered my knee badly. It will take ages to recover, if it ever does at all.'

The woman sucked her breath. 'Ah, that's too bad. I heard you were a decent player too.'

I smiled shyly. 'Not as good as some.' I gestured towards Alice who was walking back towards us. 'Luckily for you, you will still be playing with the best.'

Alice was holding up her list proudly. She looked like a sergeant major about to read out a roll-call.

Like Mr Frankland said – she was the perfect captain.

'Thank you so much for coming today, ladies,' she said loudly. 'As you can appreciate, it has been difficult to come to a decision. So many of you show talent and promise – and that in itself impressed us.' She paused, her eyes passing across the crowd. 'I want to say how much it means to me – to us – to have seen so many of you come to this trial, to want to try out for our football team. It makes me realise how important and special our team is. It also makes me realise how many good footballers we already have out there. If you haven't been selected today, please do not despair. Come to our training sessions. Help yourself become a better a player. Be part of our wonderful team, because we want you here beside us.'

There was a ripple of applause and a murmur of agreement in the crowd.

Alice beamed. 'Now – with no further ado, let me tell you our team selection. In no particular order, the women who have been chosen to play against Coulthard Foundry are as follows: Alice Standing, Elise Nixon, Florrie Rance, Gertie Whittle, Florrie Redford, Lily Jones, Maggie Kay, Bella Traynor, Evelyn Clayton and Elizabeth Berkins.'

There was a great whooping and cheering at the news. Girls were swept up in hugs of congratulations and one girl – I think it was Bella Traynor – had almost been crying when her name was read out. The energy was overwhelming. I stared up at Alice and could see how excited she looked. Her eyes were shining with joy and she had to dab at her own tears at the end of her announcement.

Mr Frankland stepped forward and patted Alice on the arm. 'Of course, you neglected one name on the list there, Alice – your own!'

The group whooped again and I saw Alice's cheeks flush red. She hated attention being drawn to her.

'Alice is an integral part of the team,' Mr Frankland

continued. 'As your captain, you can rely on her character and good influence to lead you to success.'

The girls roared their agreement. I found my own eyes tearing up again at the belief that they had in the team and in Alice.

Mr Frankland held up his hand to indicate that he meant to continue and when the silence was granted, he spoke again. 'This is the start of an exciting and, I believe, unique journey. I have witnessed talent and strength in you women that many men lack. This is your chance to show the public what you are capable of. This is your chance to play the beautiful game.'

The crowd roared again, but this time me and Alice joined in – probably louder than anyone else.

'This is your chance,' he repeated. 'Your chance to be part of the change.'

As I was going to leave, Mr Frankland approached me. I could see his cheeks were still pink from the cold and excitement, but he had at least made an attempt to re-comb his hair. As he strode over to me, I noticed how relaxed and confident he appeared with his shoulders drawn back and his head held high. He looked like a man who had just discovered a thousand pounds.

'Hettie,' he called. 'I hope you don't mind – I wanted a quick word.'

'Not at all, Mr Frankland.'

'Good, good . . . So, now that Alice has confirmed a team, we can really get things moving. I've already arranged that we can play at Deepdale. A meeting will be held on Tuesday with the Preston North End board, but I'm confident that they will pass the motion.' He paused. 'We may have to pay a charge of course, for use of the ground, but I'm hoping that they will waiver that in the spirit of generosity.'

'And if they don't?' I queried.

Mr Frankland shrugged good-naturedly. 'I'm sure we can find the money somewhere, Hettie. After all, this is all for a good cause. We are raising money for poorly soldiers – who in their right mind would want to stop us?'

I nodded, taking some comfort in his words, but there was still an uneasy feeling inside of me. I found myself peering down at my feet, which were kicking the ground restlessly.

'Are you quite all right, Hettie?' Mr Frankland asked gently. 'I don't mean to pry, of course, but I assumed that you would be a little more upbeat than this. It is an exciting time for the ladies' team.'

'I know,' I muttered. 'And I am proud, I really am.'

'But your thoughts are elsewhere?'

'I . . .'

I shook my head, feeling quite ashamed of my thoughts. 'I just wish I could be part of it. That's all.'

Mr Frankland sighed softly. 'You know you still can be, don't you, Hettie? The girls still want you to be part of the team and so do I. You could help me. You could–'

'Thank you, Mr Frankland,' I said sharply. 'But I still don't think I can.' Not unless I wanted to suffer my dad's rage for ever more.

I knew I had no other choice but to walk away from all this. The thought of that made me feel sick and hopeless, but it was just how it was.

Despite what Freddie and the others said, I had to accept my lot. It wasn't worth the anger and upset I would cause if I didn't.

'Ah – all right.' He nodded slowly. 'But if you ever change your mind . . .'

I smiled sadly back, only wishing I could.

'Is that all, Hettie? Is there something else troubling you?'

I glanced up. Mr Frankland was peering down at me with that kindly, knowing stare of his. He nodded gently and then sighed. 'Ah – I thought as much. Are you thinking of your brother? Of Freddie? I heard you visited him the other day.'

'I am thinking of him, sir,' I said. 'I find it hard to stop. I keep remembering how thin and pale he looked in that hospital bed. He was quite unlike the brother I remembered . . .'

'But he is still your brother,' Mr Frankland said firmly. 'And a fine one at that.'

'The nurse there said that he might be broken in ways we can't see . . .' I couldn't help but shudder. 'What if that's the case? What if he's never the same again?'

Mr Frankland stepped back a little and tipped his head slightly towards the sky. 'Hettie – do you believe in spirit?'

I paused. 'I'm not sure. I think so . . .'

'Spirit is what makes us who we are,' he continued, still looking towards the sky. 'It's spirit that made Grace want to start a ladies' football team, against the odds. It's spirit that keeps hope burning in those cold, dark trenches where men see sights they never want to speak of again.'

'And Freddie's spirit?' I whispered. 'It's still the same?'

'It might be wavering. It might be dulled. But no matter how broken a person becomes, his spirit is still the same. Do you see?' Mr Frankland turned back to me and smiled. 'Your brother will need time. He might need space. But he will return to you. His spirit is still there.'

'Just like he promised,' I said softly.

'Just like he promised,' he repeated.

Later on, in bed, Martha asked me to repeat the story of the trials for a third time. Below us we could hear the rise and fall of Mam and Dad's voices. Dad hadn't long been in from the pub and his words were particularly loud and cruel tonight. I only wished I could block them out for both of us.

'I can't, Martha dear,' I replied. 'I'm so tired. I need to sleep.'

'I want you to tell me about Lily Jones again – was she really good?'

'She was, Martha, one of the best. So quick and sharp. Like a whippet.'

'And Gertie?'

'She scored some wonderful goals. I told you this.'

Martha nestled against me. 'I want to see it for myself, Hettie. I want to watch them play.'

'And you will,' I promised her. 'You will, one day . . .'

The front door slammed, rattling the entire house, and

deep in the depths of downstairs I could hear my mam's frustrated sobs.

'Where has he gone now?' Martha whispered.

'Back to the pub, I expect,' I muttered.

'Why does he hate it here so?' she continued, her breath tickling against my arm. 'Whenever he's home, he's angry and shouts.'

'I don't know . . .' I said. 'He wasn't always like this. Mam says it's the pain. His job. The worry . . .'

But these were just guesses, of course. I did not know the real reason.

I thought of Mr Frankland's words, of the comfort he had given me. But was it possible that he could be wrong?

Was Dad's spirit broken so badly that it could never be fixed?

'And so, Mr Frankland concluded that the Preston North End board must've been in a generous mood when they met on Tuesday, as they've decided to waiver the five-pound charge for use of their ground.'

'That's amazing, Hettie,' Freddie said, sitting up straighter. 'What else did the board say?'

I was so pleased that Freddie was as impressed as I was with the board's reaction to the proposed Dick, Kerr Girls' charity match. It had gone so much better than Mr Frankland had dared to hope. As a result, he couldn't stop talking about it all day in the office. Even though I still felt sad to no longer be involved, I was excited for the girls.

'The match will be played on Christmas Day,' I told Freddie. 'They've even said the game can be advertised on the Preston North End posters, as long as the factory stumps up the cost. Mr Frankland doesn't seem to think that will be a problem.'

'Fame and fortune indeed.' Freddie beamed.

'Indeed. The match is becoming quite high profile,

Freddie. Mr Frankland is expecting it to be advertised in the local paper as being a Great Holiday Attraction – how wonderful is that? If that doesn't draw the crowds in, I don't know what will!'

'It really is good news,' he agreed. 'And do you know what's even better?'

'What?' I looked at him curiously.

'Matron says that I should be able to leave here in a few days.'

'Oh, Freddie!' I reached forward and took his hand in mine, squeezing it tight. 'That's such wonderful news.'

'It is, isn't it?' He grinned. 'I mean, it will take a while until I'm fully back on my feet again, but I've been practising a fair bit with the cane. Mam says I can sleep downstairs in her bed until I'm right again.'

'So Mam and Dad will be in our room?' I shuddered a little, thinking of Dad's snoring, but it was a small price to pay to have Freddie home again.

'I could go to the match with you, if you'd like?' he said. 'I would like to go, and it would be nice to have some company.'

'Oh.' I paused, my skin prickling at the thought. I wondered if Freddie had any idea how much I wanted to see that game. He always had a way of knowing what was inside of my head. 'Oh, Freddie, I'd love that. But Dad won't allow it. He said I am to have nothing more to do with the girls.'

Freddie snorted. 'Dad says these things in rage, often without thinking. What harm will it do, going to one match? I've heard there will be plenty of women going. The nurses here have all been talking about it.'

'Really?' I said, shocked.

'Really! Matron is a big fan. She will be pleased to know there is a confirmed date.'

'And you don't mind taking me with you?'

I did wonder if Dad would be happier if I were to go with Freddie, if somehow that would be more acceptable. After all, he would still need looking after. He could hardly go on his own . . .

As if reading my mind, Freddie said, 'I'll need you with me, Hettie. I'm still unsteady on my feet, and I'll need a hand getting there.'

I nodded. All right. Why not?

Freddie squeezed my hand again. 'You're not to worry about our daft dad,' he muttered. 'He'll see sense in the end.'

I leant forward on my chair. It was busy in the hospital today. The rise and fall of the men's voices was much louder than normal and in the next bed, I could hear Micky Adams groaning softly as a nurse attended to him.

'How is he doing?' I whispered, tipping my head towards his drawn curtain.

Freddie frowned a little. 'Not too good, poor lad. I try talking to him, but it doesn't work. He simply lies in that bed, staring at the ceiling. Sometimes he cries out, but most of the time he's completely silent. I'm not even sure he knows who I am any more.'

'How awful.'

Freddie snorted. 'It is what it is, Hettie. We are paying the price for fighting. I—'

He was forced to stop talking as another attack of coughing overtook him. I watched as his thin frame fought against each violent thrust. He rammed his hand up against his mouth and blinked away angry tears. 'I can't be like this for ever, Hettie. I won't let myself be like this for ever.'

'I know.' I patted his leg, which was cloaked under a thick, rough blanket. 'How are the dreams?'

'Still bad.' He wouldn't look at me. He never did when we spoke of this. 'I wake up and sometimes I'm still half-trapped inside them. There's smoke; gas all around me and a man is shouting . . .'

He stopped and shifted on the bed so that my hand fell on to the flat mattress.

'We shouldn't talk of this, lass, and please do not breathe a word to Mam and Dad. I will be all right. I will manage.' He coughed again. 'I'd rather listen to your stories – they brighten my day, they really do.'

'I'm glad,' I replied, pleased that I was of some help. It was so hard to sit here and watch my brother struggle. I felt so useless.

'How is your knee?' he asked me suddenly.

'It still pains me if I stand for too long, let alone attempt to run.' I paused. 'It makes me so sad that I can no longer play a part in the team. They're moving on without me, which I know is a good thing for them – but it still hurts.'

'You will play a part,' Freddie said. 'You'll see. You're important to them too.'

I blushed. 'I don't know, Freddie. Maybe.' I smiled shyly. 'Although . . . Grace did say that once you are part of the Dick, Kerr family you never really leave . . . Do you think she could be right?'

'I do.' He nodded firmly. 'And you are part of that family, Hettie. Don't ever forget it. Family is everything. Dad once said that, did you know?'

'Did he?' I frowned. 'I don't remember.'

'He did, long ago before his dark moods overtook him. He used to say that family was all that mattered – that you had to look after your own.'

'I never knew that,' I said.

'Dad has a good heart really.' Freddie coughed sharply. 'He just tries very hard to disguise it. Maybe it's the last thing he wants to protect.'

'Protect? Protect it from what?'

'Hurt.'

By the time I got home, it was quite late. Darkness had cloaked our street and the night air had the wintery scent of smoke and ice. I slipped into the house, keen to eat quickly and take myself upstairs to bed. I was exhausted after work and from visiting Freddie. My entire body was aching, but my knee in particular was throbbing.

I expected the house to be quiet. I knew Mam was due to visit our neighbour, Mrs Daniels, for their weekly gossip and sewing session. Martha would already be tucked up in bed, fast asleep.

'Hettie.'

I turned, surprised to find Dad standing by the kitchen door. For a moment I wondered if I was later than I thought, but Dad's stable and upright stance suggested that he hadn't been to the pub this evening and I couldn't smell the stale stink of beer on his breath.

'How is he?' Dad asked.

'Freddie?' I paused briefly. 'He's bearing up. His leg still troubles him, and he has a nasty cough from the gas, but he's getting stronger.'

Dad's eyes widened. 'Is he?'

'Yes, I believe he is.'

Dad sighed and slumped a little against the doorframe. 'That's good then, isn't it? My boy. He'll soon be back. Back on his feet.'

'Dad? Are you all right?'

'All right? Of course I'm all right.' His voice drifted. 'I'm just worried for the lad, that's all.'

'You could always go and visit him,' I offered.

Dad froze for a moment, his head slightly bowed. 'Aye, I could,' he said finally. 'But I doubt the lad will want to see me.'

'I think he would love to see you,' I said quietly. 'He's coming home soon, Dad. That's good news, isn't it?'

Dad didn't reply, but his head lowered further.

I walked up to him. Dad was never a large man, but he seemed smaller slumped up against the door frame – almost half his size. 'Dad, are you sure you're all right?'

He lifted his head. His eyes were blazing in the light. He sighed.

'All right? Hettie, love, I've not been all right for some time now.' He reached out and touched my face. It was a gentle touch, not one I was used to, and it made me gasp a little. 'I'm a silly fool, that's what I am. A silly, old fool.'

'Dad . . .'

'Don't you worry about me.' His fingers stroked my cheek. 'Tell Freddie I'm looking forward to him coming home.'

'You could tell him that yourself, Dad,' I said. 'Honestly, he would love to see you. He really would.'

'I'm not sure that's true, Hettie.' His hand left my cheek and fluttered back down to his side. 'If you can learn anything from me, love, learn not to be stubborn. It never helps anyone. It only leads to more problems.'

'Dad . . .'

But he had already begun to walk away.

It was the Saturday that Freddie was due home. I took Martha to the shops with me to collect some essentials that Mam wanted for his return. She was already in such a flap about it, cleaning the house from top to bottom and shooing me and Martha away. It was quite a relief to get away, to be honest.

I also knew the girls would be training today. I had been walking over to the field at Ashton Park to watch them, without Dad knowing. However, today I wasn't that disappointed to be missing the session; there was only so much standing around in the cold a girl could tolerate. Most of the time I simply felt sad and downhearted about not being able to join in. Now and again, I had attempted to jog lightly on the spot, but the jarring pain in my knee soon stopped me.

'Even Freddie seems to be improving quicker than me,' I grumbled to Martha as we traipsed down the road. I knew this was terribly unfair, as Freddie was struggling to walk with his new cane and still pulled up short when the pain in his leg became too much. But I felt envious that he was progressing, while I was doing nothing of the sort.

'I feel so useless,' I muttered. 'What am I going to do now?'

Martha was searching my face with her bright, knowing stare. She was such a clever child for her age. Everyone said so. 'Maybe you haven't found the thing you're meant to do yet,' she said. 'It might happen soon. You might find something else you're good at and the problem will be solved.'

'Perhaps . . .'

But I wasn't convinced.

We stepped into the greengrocers. Mam never had much money to give us, but she always insisted that we buy some apples if we could and also some carrots and greens for her to add to the stew. I knew she was finding it hard, especially with the shortages we had due to the war. The limits on sugar meant that Mam couldn't make us the usual Christmas treats. The entire country was struggling, not just us.

I immediately breathed in the lovely, fresh scent as we entered the shop. It was like our own piece of the countryside. For a moment or so, you could believe you were someplace else. Somewhere far away from the city smoke and grime.

Mrs Dawson was behind the counter and greeted us in

her usual bright fashion. Then she continued gossiping with two other women that I didn't recognise, but from the nature of their conversation, I guessed they were local. One was a large lady, dressed in a fine dark coat and dressy hat. The other woman was smaller, with a nervous look upon her thin, drawn face.

'And so the game is on Christmas Day, I hear – at Preston's main ground.'

My ears pricked up and I moved nearer to the women, pretending to be suddenly interested in Mrs Dawson's newly acquired Brussels sprouts.

'Can you believe it? Women playing football? It's quite a shock,' the thin woman hissed, her lips pursed together. 'Do you think they'll have their legs on show?'

'I should hope not, Edna. There will be outrage,' Mrs Dawson replied confidently.

'People expect women to act and behave in a certain manner. Not running around on the grass getting all sweaty and ugly,' the lady named Edna replied, pulling what was, ironically, quite an ugly face.

'I've heard they won't even be wearing corsets! Can you imagine!' added Mrs Dawson. 'It doesn't seem very proper. Or safe. Surely they could do themselves some harm!'

'Indeed! What will they even be wearing?'

'I've heard the ladies will be wearing shorts, just like the men. And what of it?'

All the women stared towards the large lady in the hat, who had suddenly spoken. She smiled broadly when she realised the attention was on her.

'Well, I think it's most inappropriate, Gladys,' Edna said, pursing her lips together.

Gladys laughed merrily. 'Oh my, Edna Saunders, have you got nowt else to grumble about? I think it's wonderful that these young girls will be going out there and showing the whole of Preston what they can do. Good for them, I say!'

'I have heard they are rather good . . .' Mrs Dawson said quietly.

'That's right, they are good, aren't they, Hettie?' Martha said suddenly, in her excited way. 'My sister knows because she's been involved with the team.'

Suddenly all eyes were on me. I gulped down my apprehension.

'Yes – yes, that's right. The team will play in the men's kit. They have to. They couldn't possibly move well properly in longer skirts. It wouldn't suit the nature of the game. And corsets would be too restrictive, they wouldn't be able to breathe properly as they run.'

'See!' Gladys puffed out her chest proudly. 'It all makes perfect sense to me. I think us women should be out there supporting them, not gossiping and mithering!'

Edna stepped forward. She looked a bit ashamed.

'Perhaps I was hasty. I was only saying what I heard, that's all,' she said, patting my arm gently.

'Yes, you were hasty,' Gladys replied firmly. 'And I tell you what, I will be going to the match and I will be cheering these ladies on. I hope you both will too. After all, we are about to witness a group of women taking on a man's game. Something we've always been told we can't do.' She giggled softly to herself. 'Who wouldn't love to see the men be proven wrong?'

'Well . . .' said Mrs Dawson. 'If it shuts my Eric up, it could well be worth it! I'd love to see his face if this bunch of women could actually play!'

'Can they really play?' Edna asked me suspiciously.

'They can!' I assured her.

'Well,' Gladys said. 'I'd say that'll definitely be worth a watch. What do you say, Ida?'

Mrs Dawson bobbed her head up and down in agreement. 'Oh aye – I reckon it'll be well worth it.'

Gladys nodded in approval. It was only as she moved away from the counter, that I saw the badge neatly pinned to her lapel. I recognised the sharp colours of purple, white and green instantly. She was a suffragette!

She winked as she passed me. 'Good luck, lassie,' she whispered under her breath.

A warm feeling eased through me.

The girls really were going to prove people wrong. They were going to make people stand up and think. And yes, maybe I wasn't directly part of that any more, but I could still make sure their message got out there.

I could help to make sure people knew the truth about the Dick, Kerr Girls.

Mam was frantic when we got home. The entire place stunk of bleach and carbolic soap; I swear she had already cleaned the house from top to bottom, five times over. Her face was red from the exertion and her hair was clammy and stuck against her face in sweaty clumps.

'Mam! Anyone would think the king himself was visiting!'

Mam glared back at me. 'Well, he may as well be. Freddie is our king. I want this house looking ship-shape for his return. After being in that awful hospital for so long, he must be crying to come home.'

'Mam! It was hardly awful!'

I thought the hospital had done a splendid job with their limited resources, keeping the soldiers clean and comfortable and making their recovery as easy as possible.

Mam pushed a lock of hair behind her ear and sighed. 'You know very well what I mean. After all, there's no place like home.'

'I thought maybe you would be there to fetch him,' I said, knowing how much Mam liked to be in control of these things.

'He didn't want that. He said he wanted to make his own way. The nurses have arranged a car to bring him, which I think was rather nice of them.' Mam's eyes moved towards the door. 'I had half a hope that your father might be home by now, but never mind.'

'He'll be working late,' I said.

Or soothing himself with another quick pint down the pub.

It looked as though some things would never change.

Freddie stood motionless in the living room for a while, his suitcase still in his hand. Then a tiny smile crept up on his face.

'Oh, this house. This smell – everything. You really don't know how much I've missed it all.'

Martha ran towards him and threw her arms around his waist. 'Freddie! We've missed you being here!' she said into the folds of his clothes.

Freddie stroked the top of her head. 'Me too, our kid. There was many a night I spent dreaming of being back here. I even missed the sound of the dripping guttering and the smell of Mam's boiled cabbage.'

'Oi! You cheeky begger!' Mam scolded, but we could see she was smiling.

'So, where's Dad then?' he asked.

Mam sighed. 'I reckon he'll be home soon enough, son.'

Freddie eased himself into the chair by the door. 'Once he's had a pint or two, eh?'

I caught his eye. He winked. He was trying to make out that he didn't mind, but of course he did. He felt the same as me. Why did Dad need a drink inside of him to face anything? Were we really that bad?

'How's your leg?' Mam asked him. 'I've got some cream that's meant to be good for all sorts of wounds. And Betty across the street swears by steam for your chest – she reckons if we boil the kettle and get you to sit by it, the heat will open your lungs right up.'

Freddie held his hands up. 'Mam – don't fuss. I'll be

all right. I need rest, that's all. I'm not as bad as many.'

Micky Adams. I arched an eyebrow. 'How is he?'

Freddie knew who I was talking about straight away. 'He's still not talking. Still cries at night.' He paused. 'I plan to visit the poor lad. His family live so far away.'

'I don't want you upsetting yourself,' Mam said.

'I won't be. I just want to help.' His voice suddenly sounded bitter. 'Do my bit.'

We were all surprised by the sound of the front door crashing open. I guess we all expected Dad to stay later in the pub. Once he went, he was usually rooted there for the rest of the night.

'Hello!' he called, before striding into the room.

My first thought was that he looked remarkably sober again. There was no swagger or sway to his walk and his cheeks weren't dark red and shiny. His eyes fell on Freddie and his smile dropped a little. I noticed how he took in the sight. I realised that this had been the first time Dad had seen Freddie since he left for war.

'Son . . .' Dad's mouth hung open for a second. He gripped the door frame. 'You look so skinny. Have you been eating at all?'

'Some . . .' Freddie pulled himself up and hobbled over to Dad. 'It's good to see you.'

Dad took his shoulders and held him. Then he brought Freddie's head against his chest and clasped it there. His face was ghost-like.

'My boy,' he whispered. 'My poor, poor boy. What did they do to you?'

Freddie eased himself away. 'I'm all right Dad, really, I am. Look at me.' He pulled on Dad's arm, forcing him to look at his face. 'I'm here. I'm all right. I got back, just like I promised.'

Dad reached forward and took Freddie's face between his hands. He looked at him, really studied him, like he was a painting or some rare piece of artwork that he'd never seen before.

'I couldn't come home,' Dad muttered. 'I walked and walked. I was so scared, isn't that daft. I was so scared of what I would see.'

'It's not daft at all, Dad.'

'But you're right. You're home. You're back with us.' His hand carefully stroked Freddie's face. 'My boy is home.'

Mam made Freddie's favourite dinner – meat pie. She had stewed the meat all day so that it wasn't too tough or gristly and the pastry was perfect – golden and cooked to perfection. I ate it quickly, wondering where my sudden hunger had come from.

'That's it. Lap it up,' Mam said, smiling at Freddie. 'There'll be no more fancy food now until Christmas Day.'

'It's lovely, Mam,' Freddie said, smiling, although I noticed he seemed to be struggling with his large portion. I wondered if he had got used to the hospital rations. Perhaps his stomach had shrunk a little.

Mam turned her attention to me, obviously keen to keep conversation flowing at the dinner table for once. I wondered if this was for Freddie's benefit.

'I saw you writing a letter today,' she said brightly. 'Who was that for?'

'Grace,' I replied slowly.

'Grace?' Dad looked up suddenly. Gravy was dribbling down his chin and he quickly wiped it away. 'Is she one of the girls from the factory?'

'She was,' I said. 'She had to leave because her health was getting worse. She's moved to the country for a bit.'

'Was she one of this footballing lot?' Dad probed, his fork stabbing into his pie.

'Yes.' I paused. 'You could say Grace started the Dick, Kerr Girls – she was the one who challenged the lads to the first game, after all. She is such a good player.'

Was such a good player . . . I bowed my head. What was it that she said in her last letter to me? She was too frail now – too old, too busy. Would Grace ever play again?

'They're all talking about it, down at the docks,' Dad muttered. 'The men – all gassing about this game that'll be played. They say there are posters up at Marsh Lane. It's being treated like a proper match.'

'That's because it is a proper match.'

'Well, we'll soon see, won't we,' said Freddie evenly. 'Because I'm taking Hettie.'

'Not fair!' Martha squealed. 'I want to go.'

'Next time, Martha,' Freddie soothed.

Dad was now sat up straight, his attention fully fixed on Freddie. 'What are you going on about, lad? You're taking Hettie? I don't want her going to that game.'

Freddie laid down his fork calmly. 'I want to see what all the fuss is about, that's all. I need Hettie's help getting there. I don't expect you want me to take you?'

Dad snorted. 'No, I don't. You couldn't pay me to see that nonsense.'

'Well then – I'm taking Hettie,' Freddie replied. 'It's a one-off. You can't begrudge her that.'

Dad looked flustered, but he held up his hands in defeat. 'Fine then! One game, but that's it.' He turned to face me. 'But I don't want you getting any ideas after it. You hear me?'

'I won't,' I replied. 'I'm just pleased to be going to a proper match.'

Dad scoffed. 'Proper match, eh? Next you'll be telling me that this team of girls will fill up the stands. That thousands of men will be chanting their names, like they do for the proper teams.'

I blinked back at him. 'Well – why shouldn't they?'

He sighed, looking at me in a pitying sort of way. 'Ah, Hettie, you just don't understand. Football has always been a man's game. It's our form of release after a long day. We gather in those cold stands and we roar for our boys. We scream for our boys. God knows, sometimes we even cry for our boys. It's something a woman will never be part of.'

'S*hould* never be part of, you mean,' Mam snapped. 'Here, Hettie, help me with these plates.'

I stood, gathering up mine and Martha's plates. I noticed that Martha was frowning at Dad in a confused manner.

'Men can cheer for the women too though, can't they?' she queried.

Dad flapped a hand dismissively. 'It's not the same.

It never will be.' His voice dropped a little. 'I don't mean to upset you, Hettie, I'm simply telling you not to expect very much. A few people will turn up on the day, aye. They will be curious. They'll want to see what all the fuss is about. But the numbers won't be good. Women's football can never be more than some daft fantasy.'

'Well, we shall see about that,' I said, crashing the plates into the sink.

Mam touched my arm. 'Oi! Watch it, love. I could do without you smashing up my dinnerware.'

'Sorry.' I turned my head away.

'Take no notice of the silly old man,' she whispered as she turned on the tap. 'What does he know? He's only gone to two football matches in his life, and one of those was when he was half-cut.'

'But what if he's right? What if no one turns up?'

'Then you try again. And you keep trying until them there stands are fit to bursting,' Mam said softly, wiping down a plate with her cloth. 'I only wish I were twenty years younger. I might have given the trial a go myself. I was quite athletic in my youth, you know. Fast, too.'

'I can believe it.' I smiled.

'I have regrets, Hettie. Don't think I don't. For so long I dreamt about seeing the world, how daft is that?

I thought I could grow up, leave Preston and get on a boat to somewhere. Sometimes, when I'm in bed at night, I still have the same dream.'

'Aw, Mam. I never knew that.'

'That's because I never told you. Don't get me wrong, I'm happy enough with my lot.' She turned her head towards Dad and shrugged. 'Most of the time. But the regrets eat away at you. Don't be like me, Hettie. Enjoy your life while you can. Take the opportunities that are given to you and don't let other people talk you out of them. Only you can know what is truly best for you.'

'Thank you, Mam,' I whispered.

'You have nothing to thank me for,' she shot back, looking flustered. 'I'm just saying – that's all.'

But she never realised how important her words were to me that day.

This was it! The day had come. Christmas Day was here.

The Dick, Kerr Girls were about to kick off!

They were about to show this town what they could do!

I awoke with the usual feeling of excitement in my belly, but this time it wasn't simply because it was Christmas Day. This year, it was because of the match that was about to be played. Various thoughts trickled through my brain.

Would the girls play well?

Would a crowd turn out to see them?

Would this be the first and only match the Dick, Kerr Girls would play?

I tried to shake off the last thought, seriously hoping I was wrong.

Martha was already out of bed and hopping around the room in glee, clutching the sock that had been left at the end of her bed.

'Look, Hettie! He's been!' she squealed. 'He's filled my sock.'

She thrust it under my nose so that I could see for

myself. Inside was the brightest orange I had seen, some nuts, a ha'penny piece and a tiny doll stitched from wool.

'Oh, Martha. You're so lucky,' I said, kissing the top of her head. 'That shows what a good girl you've been all year round.'

'I don't understand why Father Christmas doesn't come to you and Freddie,' Martha said, frowning a little. 'You've both been good too. Freddie especially. He's been brave.'

I ruffled her hair. 'I'm too old for such things, Martha. Father Christmas is far too busy serving all the little children in the country and it's right that he should.'

'I love Christmas!' Martha declared.

I grinned back. 'So do I!'

The morning flew past in a wonderful medley of laughter and noise. The neighbours popped in to wish us festive greetings and even Dad seemed relaxed, drinking a glass of port that one of them brought over as a gift. Mam kept herself busy in the kitchen but was singing softly under her breath, seemingly lost in her own little world. Freddie had already started one of the new books he'd been given. Martha was delighted with her present – a lovely cuddly teddy bear, who she immediately named Clarence – and I loved the black boots that Mam and Dad had given me. They were so shiny and new, compared to my old ones. I would no longer feel ashamed wearing my tatty ones to work.

But as much as I loved being with my family when they were so relaxed and happy for once, my eyes kept on scanning the large clock in the living room. I couldn't wait for the afternoon to come. It was almost as if I could hear my own football whistle in my head and I knew when it blew, it was time to run.

But of course, I didn't run. I couldn't. I had to walk slowly and carefully with Freddie. We were a right pair. Him with his bad leg and walking stick, and me with my gammy knee, which still meant I couldn't walk fast and struggled on uneven surfaces.

We held each other as we moved forward, a shambolic, lopsided kind of movement down the cobbled streets. Thankfully it wasn't a long way and the buzz of excitement within both of us meant that we could ignore our pain a little.

'Thanks for this,' I whispered to Freddie.

He simply smiled back at me. 'I think I will probably end up thanking you.'

As soon as we turned the corner, we saw the first signs of crowds. A gaggle of men were easing their way towards

Preston's ground. I paused for a second in the street, slightly confused. We weren't even on the main street that led into the stadium, yet already there were people in the street, football scarves draped around their necks, rattles in their hands. This was a perfectly normal sight for a men's game.

But this wasn't a men's game!

'Look at them all!' I breathed.

'They're all here for the girls!' Freddie said keenly. 'This is certainly going to be a well-supported game.'

We continued walking, passing the large group, weaving our way towards the ground. As we walked, we passed more and more people. Men and women. They all looked so jolly and excited, dressed in bright colours and talking merrily.

'What a sight this will be!' one woman said, nudging me as I passed her. 'I've heard both teams are good. Who will win, I wonder?'

'From what I've heard, our Dick, Kerr ladies beat a group of men recently,' a large man boomed. 'They are the ones to watch.'

He said '*our* ladies'. Not 'the ladies', or 'those ladies' – '*our* ladies'!

By the time we reached the ground, I was buzzing with pride.

As we approached the gates, Freddie gently nudged me in the side.

'Isn't that one of your teammates?' he asked.

I followed his gaze.

He was right. Standing by the railings, all on her own, was Alice.

As soon as I walked over to her, she grabbed my hands.

'Oh, Hettie. I was looking for you. I hoped to see you,' she said quickly. I noticed how pale her face was, and how her hands quivered under my grip.

'Are you all right?' I asked her.

'I just – I'm just . . .' She blinked at me. 'I'm just nervous, that's all. The girls all rely on me. They all hope so much that we can play well today.' She sighed and I felt the shiver run through her body. 'People are expecting so much. They want to see us play well. What if . . .'

'You will play well,' I told her firmly.

'But I'm not Grace. Without her here . . .'

'Grace believed in you. She believed in all of us.' I lowered my voice. 'And Grace is here with us too. You know that.'

Alice nodded.

'I'm here. I'm going to be cheering you on. I'm right by your side.'

Alice looked up, tears brimming in her eyes. 'Please

come in with us, Hettie. I want you there. I want you to walk out on the pitch with us. I want you on the sidelines with Mr Frankland, shouting support.'

'But why?' I shook my head. 'What difference do I make?'

'You're one of us,' she giggled. 'You're our lucky charm. I dunno – whatever it is, we need you there. Please come in with me.'

I looked over at Freddie, but he simply waved me off dismissively.

'I'll be fine, Hettie. You got me here, that's all that matters. And I got you here.' His eyes twinkled. 'Now hurry up. Your girls need you. There's a job to be done.'

In the dressing room, everyone was electric with nerves. You could sense the tension from across the room as the girls jostled to get ready, joking loudly among themselves that this was a Christmas Day with a difference.

'Can you believe we are actually here? In a proper stadium?' Lily Jones shouted. 'Look at us! Isn't it queer?'

'My brother was joking that I should be in the kitchen, washing up the dinner plates,' Alice Kell replied loudly. 'He didn't like the kick in the shin I gave him for saying that!'

The girls roared with laughter.

'My dad is going to buy me a new dress if I score today,' Florrie Rance said loudly. She stared down bleakly at her borrowed football boots, which were a little oversized. 'I know what I'd rather have! It fact, I'll tell him as much if I get a goal.'

'Don't we all!' said Gertie, holding her own battered boot in the air – one of her brother's cast-offs. 'Look at the state of this! And it stinks a bit too!'

Everyone burst into laughter. Yet still the nervous tension was there, like a gentle wave washing over all of us. Each girl slowly got themselves prepared, dressing in the smart but oversized black-and-white-striped kit, complete with neat black hats. Then each girl took turns stretching and easing out their muscles.

'This is so much easier to do without a corset,' Florrie Redford pointed out, moving her body freely from side to side. 'I actually feel like I can breathe.'

'Hear, hear!' Gertie said, kicking her discarded corset across the room. 'I'm glad to see the back of the thing. It's like being an enclosed animal!'

It wasn't long at all until we were filing down the long, bright tunnel.

I walked alongside Alice, who was leading the way, clutching the bucket and sponge in case there were any injuries I could help with. Strangely the pain in my knee had subsided, only to be replaced by a buzzing sensation in my stomach. I reckon – if I'd been asked – I could've run on to the pitch, if only for a few seconds. My God, how I would've loved that!

Inside the tunnel, we could hear the noise of the crowd. What a sound! It seemed to overtake everything else.

'Listen to that!' one of the women said. 'Oh my – just listen. They're all out there waiting for us to start. What if . . .'

She didn't finish the words, but we knew she was thinking what we all feared. What if this went wrong? What if we made a show of ourselves? What if we couldn't do this?

Alice paused for a second, drinking in the noise. Then, with a smile on her face, she turned around and addressed the team in her usual calm and assured manner. She was back to her old self now.

'Come on, girls, we can do it! Just remember – this is for the soldiers!'

'For the soldiers, yes!' Florrie Redford repeated.

The girls all cheered in reply and pumped their fists.

'And for Grace,' I said. 'This is for her, too.'

I'd like to think that somehow she heard me.

I stood on the sidelines, hardly able to believe where I was. As a girl, it felt wrong to be standing at the side of a famous football pitch. Despite my best efforts, a voice still nagged in my head. 'You don't belong here. None of you belong here. This is no place for a girl.'

I shook my head determinedly. I couldn't listen to that voice. Not today. Instead, I looked around me, still not quite able to believe the sight. The stadium looked almost full. One of the stewards had whispered that there were ten thousand people here, maybe more. I hadn't believed him at first, but looking around now, I did. The stands were full of bodies. People cheering and roaring with anticipation for the game.

The place was alive with noise and excitement. It was clear that the crowd were looking for entertainment after their hearty Christmas dinners.

After a brief warm up, the players nervously took their positions. The referee beckoned the captains towards the centre circle to shake hands and toss a coin to decide which team kicked off – and it was us! The noise from the crowd built steadily in anticipation, and as the captains returned to their positions, Florrie prepared to take the centre. The ref had one last check to make sure both keepers were ready and, with a raise of the hand, he blew his whistle. The crowd roared their approval, and we were off!

Coulthard, dressed in their bright red-and-white stripes, started the game quite sheepishly. Strangely, so did the Dick, Kerr Girls. It was almost as if both teams were rather scared of making the first attack. But it wasn't long before Alice's screamed instructions brought the team together and the Dick, Kerr Girls began to move forward.

Mr Frankland stood next to me, his arms folded in front of him, rocking nervously back and forth on his heels.

'Come on, girls!' he shouted. 'Move the ball forward, that's it. Show them what you're made of.'

We certainly looked the stronger side and players like Alice Kell were easily able to dispossess the opposition and keep the advantage. Lily, Flo and Florrie Rance were fast in the attack and sharp with the ball with Elizabeth Berkins hanging just behind them, waiting for an opportunity. It wasn't long before a long ball reached Elizabeth, who moved it quickly to Florrie Rance as she raced into the six-yard area.

'Come on, Florrie!' I called, almost unable to look.

The crowd roared with excitement. I swear some of them were chanting our team's name. Florrie's shot slammed against the post before turning out for a corner. Florrie clasped her head in frustration – I wondered if she was thinking about her promised dress!

The corner was knocked in, but the Coulthard ladies were strong in defence and quickly won the ball back.

'We need another quick break,' Mr Frankland said. 'We need another chance to show our speed and skill.'

It wasn't long in coming. Another sweeping ball found Gertie Whittle in the penalty area and, with deft control, she volleyed it into the top corner. The goalkeeper, who to be fair, looked to be in reasonable shape, never stood a chance.

The crowd roared! I swear I screamed as loud as I ever have. Mr Frankland jumped up and down on the spot, waving his arms in pleasure.

'Well done, Gertie. That's how we do it!'

The Dick, Kerr Girls were now fired up and ready to show that they meant business. I could tell by the sheer confidence of their movement and the accuracy of their passing. It was something to relish! Each girl seemed to be making the right decisions and moving into the space.

It wasn't long before Elizabeth Berkins took a shot from fifteen yards. The ball sailed effortlessly through the air and swept in, just under the bar. Even Elizabeth herself seemed stunned, as she stood frozen for a moment, her mouth wide open, as the crowd exploded once again. Two-nil. This was how to do it. They were making it look so easy.

Just before half-time, Florrie Rance made it three-nil, confidently side-footing a lovely ball into the back of net and leaving the poor Coulthard goalkeeper on her bottom. Straight after, Florrie turned towards me, winked sweetly and pointed to her boots.

Maybe her gift would come through after all! She certainly deserved it!

The whistle blew for half-time and the crowd roared again, still chanting our team name. Mr Frankland and I hurried over to the team, overcome with pride and excitement.

'That was, quite frankly, excellent,' he said to Alice Kell. 'You need to mark closer and watch for gaps in defence, but you have the pace here. You can outrun them.'

'You look the better side,' I added.

Alice shook her head. 'The game isn't over yet. We mustn't get ahead of ourselves.'

On the other side of the pitch, the Coulthard girls stood in their huddle – talking through their own tactics. I saw their captain, Lily Forshaw, look over towards us. Her expression was a mix of admiration and frustration. Behind us the crowds were still merry, singing loudly and shaking their rattles in the air. It was such a joyous occasion.

'This is wonderful,' I breathed. 'It's a game to be proud of.'

After a ten-minute break, the second half began in earnest and I resumed my spot on the halfway line. Mr Frankland stood beside me, but this time he was more relaxed, with his hands thrust deep into his pockets and a lazy smile spread across his face.

The whistle blew and once again the crowd roared.

'Listen to the people, Hettie,' he muttered in amazement. 'They love this. They love us! The girls are keeping them more entertained then we could ever have believed.'

'Don't speak too soon, Mr Frankland,' I said, edging forwards. Alice's words were also replaying in my ears – *we mustn't get ahead of ourselves . . .*

The Coulthard ladies had started with a spring in their step and a gritty determination to keep possession. Despite our best efforts, it was difficult to keep the ball out of our own half. One of their players, a tall, spindly young girl with quick feet, soon had a shot on target and drew moans of protest from the Coulthard fans when her shot spun wide.

'Come on, girls!' Mr Frankland shouted, his face tensing. 'Keep the ball forward! Let's not lose it now.'

Our girls were still fighting for the ball, but the Coulthard team were showing a strength and spirit that had been lacking in the first half. A few more darting runs led them deep into our penalty area. Luckily, both Alice Kell and Margaret Kay were playing a strong game in defence and were able to make some key clearances to stop the opposition from scoring.

The crowd continued to sing loudly. This was end-to-end play and no matter who you supported, you couldn't help but be excited. Each woman on the pitch was fighting hard to prove their worth. No one was ready to surrender. This was a proper match that was worthy of the attention it was getting.

'C'mon ladies!' I called again. 'Show them what you've got!'

The half continued with no further goals, until the Coulthard ladies broke again. A winger picked up the ball in space and ran down the flank unchallenged. She was able to cross the ball into her captain, Lily Forshaw, who was waiting in the penalty area. The last defender back to mark her was Alice Kell.

The tackle came quick. I knew it was too high even before Alice had made contact and I knew Alice thought the same as both she and Lily tumbled to ground. Lily was clutching her thigh and yelling in protest – Alice was looking down at the ground, her mouth open in disappointment. The referee blew for a penalty straight away. A mixture of howls and screams filled the stadium. Beside me, Mr Frankland's head dropped a little.

'Alice will be so angry with herself for that,' he said. 'She plays with passion and spirit, but sometimes that can overspill.'

Lily Forshaw placed the ball on the penalty spot. There was deathly silence around the ground. I bowed my head, unable to look. This was sure to be a goal. Maybe it would change the entire course of the game?

Then I heard the sudden cheer from our end. I looked up to see Lily standing with her head in hands and our goalkeeper, Evelyn Clayton, clutching the ball in her safe hands.

She saved it! My God, she'd saved it! What a keeper!

Almost immediately the pace of the game changed. The Coulthard ladies' heads seemed to have dropped and they slipped back into a more defensive game. The Dick, Kerr

Girls, however, were alive now. They drove the ball forward and began to press their opponents further. It wasn't long until Florrie Redford had another shot and missed.

Coulthard picked up the ball again, this time by their young winger on the right, eager to make another break, but she was quickly dispossessed, this time cleanly, by Alice, who had seemed to have got her confidence back. The player jumped up in anger and ran towards the referee, followed by several of her teammates. I frowned. Surely they weren't protesting? It had been a clean tackle and the referee had already indicated the game should play on.

Then, while the Coulthard ladies were still protesting, Alice Kell took the ball and made a surge forward. Spotting that Florrie Rance was completely free by the goal mouth, I yelled at the top of my voice.

'Alice! Pass to Florrie! On your right!'

Alice looked up quickly in my direction and then, just as quickly, passed the ball sweetly towards Florrie who caught it on her right foot. Without hesitation, Florrie ran on to goal and netted the ball neatly in the bottom corner. The crowd roared with pleasure and Florrie beamed with pride.

No one was cheering as loud as me! As Alice ran past me, she gave me the thumbs up sign. I felt myself glow all over.

Coulthard were clearly getting rattled. They took the centre, but quickly lost possession through a misplaced pass which was picked up by Gertie Whittle. The ball was threaded through to Lily Jones who cut inside the defender and curled a shot just wide of the far post, triggering 'ooohs' and applause from the crowds. With time running out, the goalkeeper took the goal kick quickly and accidently planted the ball firmly into her teammate's torso. The young lady fell, clutching her chest, and the referee, probably not knowing what else to do – and certainly not where to look – staggered back a little and then blew his whistle for full-time. I think he was relieved that the game was over.

He wasn't the only one to be relieved!

The crowd roared with pleasure. The girls ran towards each other in glee.

And I stood there, drinking it all in.

This was an unique kind of day. It would be one I'd never forget.

I think I knew, right there in that moment, that this was the beginning of something quite special.

'Four-nil!'

'We won! We only went and bloody did it!'

'Did you see it? Florrie's goals. What goals! And Evelyn's save. What a game!'

'I swear this is the best feeling ever. I want to bottle it. It's better than gin.'

The chatter wouldn't stop in the dressing room. Everyone was beside themselves. It was hard not to be caught up in the sheer wonder of it all.

'Did you see the crowd? Did you see how many there were?'

'Never mind see – did you hear them? They were cheering for us. They were cheering everything we did.'

'We put on a show, didn't we! We showed them.'

Alice Kell was sat in the corner, watching everyone with a tired but content look on her face. I sat myself beside her and squeezed her arm.

'You did it, Alice.'

'*We* did it,' she corrected, talking out loud to the team now. 'The team did this. Each and every one of us.'

'It was so good,' I told her. 'There was so much good play. The passing, the movement . . .'

'The defence?' She looked up and winked. 'You're right, though. The training paid off. All of you worked hard. But we are women, remember – never forget that. The crowd were behind us today, but they might not be tomorrow.

They won't let us forget that we are the weaker sex. Not yet. We have to prove to them that we're not.'

'And you'll do that!' I said, grinning.

'Of course we bloody will,' Alice laughed. 'One day, women's football will be as important as men's. It really will.'

One day . . .

It was the Monday after the game, and almost time to pack up shop, when Mr Frankland called me into his office. I was a little surprised as we had already spoken at lunchtime about the work he required. Was I in some kind of trouble? It was true that my mind had not been fully on the job today. I kept reliving the match, thinking through every moment – each high and low. The other apprentices had been teasing me all morning about my dazed state.

'Look at her head in the clouds, as always.'

'Do you think she's dreaming about some fella?'

'Not likely. From what I've heard, all she worries about is that daft football team – if you can call it that.'

My cool stares and tart responses didn't seem to be working today – not that I was really bothered. I walked into Mr Frankland's office in a bit of a daze, trying to push my thoughts to the back of my mind.

'Ah!' Mr Frankland said softly. 'Take a seat there, lass, and don't be looking so down in the mouth. You're not in any trouble.'

'I'm not?' I smiled. 'Well, that's a relief. I couldn't be sure. It's been so hard to focus on things these past few days.'

'Well, that's understandable. And how is Freddie now? Is he settling back in at home?'

I nodded. 'He is.'

'Your mam must be very happy and Freddie must be so pleased.'

'Oh yes, they both are so relieved. He's still struggling to move around a bit and he doesn't like sleeping downstairs much, but I'm sure he'll get used to it.'

'It won't be for ever,' Mr Frankland replied gently. 'He'll soon be his old self.'

'Yes, I hope so.'

I didn't tell Mr Frankland that Freddie was still plagued by bad dreams. Freddie only told me about them. He didn't want anyone else to worry, but I knew they kept him awake for most of the night.

'Actually, it was Freddie I wanted to talk to you about,' Mr Frankland said. 'There's something I wanted to show you.'

'Oh?'

Mr Frankland reached into his top drawer and brought out a large black box. He placed it on the desk and nudged it towards me.

'Mr Frankland . . . I'm not sure I understand?'

He sat back on his chair, his arms resting on his stomach. 'Hettie, as you know, the Dick, Kerr Girls have been raising money for the soldiers at Moor Park Hospital. We also wanted to raise some money for one of the young lads who used to work here – in this very department.'

'What is it?' I asked, curious.

'I think that's for Freddie to find out, don't you? But I'm confident he will like it very much. I wanted you to give it to him.'

I nodded. 'But I'm not sure Freddie will accept a gift. He's very proud, you know.'

'That's as may be. But this is something that can help him fulfil his purpose, just like the girls are fulfilling theirs.'

I stroked the smooth texture of the box. 'This is so lovely of you, but . . .'

Mr Frankland smiled at me. 'It's what the boy deserves. Give it to him tonight, Hettie. Put a smile on his face. Tell him the Dick, Kerr Girls want him to succeed.'

I nodded. 'OK, I will. Hopefully it'll put a smile back on his face.'

He leant forward, his eyes wide and steady. 'I really think it will. And Hettie . . .' Mr Frankland's eyes remained fixed on mine. 'I wondered if you'd thought any more about the offer I made to you before? It still stands, you know.'

'The offer?'

'To help the team,' he replied smoothly. 'Things are going to get much busier now. I really need someone to help me deal with the enquiries, the fundraising and the general running of the club.'

'And you'd still like me to help?'

'I could think of no better person,' he replied.

I thought of Dad, of his sour words and dark warnings. But then I thought of Mam, and of how she looked at me with her earnest, intelligent eyes. How she had told me to follow my dreams. How she had almost pleaded with me to be true to myself.

I knew I couldn't keep living in my dad's shadow, nor could I keep falling into step with men. This was time for women to move forward, to take our places and show our worth. If the war had succeeded in anything, it had been to teach us that we were as worthy as any man.

And if the Dick, Kerr Girls had taught *me* anything, it was that I was able to choose a different path if I wanted to. I could live the life that I chose.

Determination rose inside of me. I was sick of holding myself back.

I wanted to be a part of this.

'I'd love to help you,' I replied firmly. 'I want to do it.'

My decision was finally made and I'd never felt happier.

We were sat, huddled together at the back of the canteen, our voices quiet amidst the hubbub around us. Flo was passing around a letter she had received from Grace.

'Isn't it lovely?' Flo said excitedly. 'She's got her Jimmy back and they're starting a new life together. She really deserves some luck.'

'She is a very special lady,' Alice said, before carefully folding the letter up and passing it back to Flo. 'Do you really think she might adopt one of those poor orphaned war children? What a wonderful thing.'

'I think that is something Grace would do,' I said quietly. 'She always does the right thing, doesn't she?'

Alice nodded. 'She really does, and I miss her very much.'

'I think I will travel down and see her,' I told them. 'One weekend perhaps. I can take some of the local news cuttings of the team that she might not have seen – and I can tell her about the possible new signings . . .'

'Oh yes, tell her about Molly Walker. Grace will be pleased with that,' Alice said.

'And tell her about Florrie Rance planning to get

married. She won't believe it – what a whirlwind!' Flo added. 'I don't think any of us were expecting that, least of all Mr Frankland. He'll be sad that she has to leave the team.'

'Don't worry – Mr Frankland has his eyes on some other girls to bolster the line-up,' Alice said. 'It'll be twice as strong before we know it. And lucky Florrie, moving away. She will have an exciting life of her own to lead now.'

'Did you see the piece in the *Lancashire Daily*?' I asked them. 'I've already kept a copy to show Grace when I see her. It lists all the money we raised for charity. Over five hundred pounds, if I remember correctly. They even said that if it were a men's team that had raised such money, it would be seen as a great achievement—'

'But as we're a women's team, it's deemed extraordinary,' Alice interjected. 'Almost beyond belief!'

'Who would have thought, eh?' Flo giggled. 'A bunch of humble women going out there and making a difference.'

'But we didn't just think it, did we?' Alice said, her eyes twinkling. 'We *did* it. And we'll continue to do it. We still have so much to prove.'

Flo touched my arm lightly. 'Will you consider training with us again, Hettie? Maybe your leg will get stronger if you do?'

'Maybe I'll try again one day,' I said. 'But if not, it doesn't matter. I'm rather happy as I am. I was never going to be a great player like you girls are, but, well – Mr Frankland has asked me to be his assistant and I've agreed. He wants me to help with administration of the team, especially now that it's getting bigger. He's fairly useless at that side of it, so I think he could do with my help.'

The girls chuckled.

'That's wonderful news,' Alice said. 'We couldn't do this without you.'

I smiled back. 'Well – like you said before – we're a team, aren't we?'

'A family,' Alice corrected. 'And Hettie, you'll always be part of ours.'

Despite the late afternoon shadows casting across the street by the time I got home, the boys were still playing out. Their football clattered down the street as they roared and cried out with joy. I was glad to see at least this time they had a new ball, albeit a flat one, instead of that old tin can. Ronnie and Davey Marshall were at one side of the street, while Will Mercer was fighting to tackle Timmy. Both of them were edging dangerously close to Mr Gibbons's rickety old fence.

'All right, Hettie!' Ronnie called out, spotting me. 'Wanna play?'

'I'd better not,' I called back.

'Your sister was playing with us for a bit, before she was called in.'

I laughed. 'I hope she gave you a run for your money.'

'She's as quick as a cat and pretty tough, too.' Ronnie grinned. 'I can't think who she gets that from.'

I was about to say something back, when Timmy hollered for Ronnie to receive his pass. Absorbed back into the game again, Ronnie waved quickly at me and ran towards the ball. I stood for a moment, just watching. It was fast, clumsy play but it was entertaining to watch. Especially when Davey attempted to tackle his brother – the two just ended up in a fist fight.

'Quite a different type of game, isn't it?'

I looked up. Dad was standing beside me.

'Dad . . . I didn't see you there.'

'Sorry. Did I make you start?'

I smiled weakly. 'A little. I thought you were at work today?'

He shook his head sadly. 'Not today, love, my back hurts too much. I had to give it a rest.' He paused. 'I've been over there by the house, watching. In fact, I've been watching ever since I called Martha in. They're quite an enthusiastic bunch of lads, aren't they? Apart from that one kid,' – he pointed absently at Ronnie – 'I don't see much talent in any of them.'

'Part of the fun is just in the play,' I said quietly. 'You don't always have to be the best player. It's about being part of a team. Being part of something.'

'Aye . . .' Dad nodded. 'I know all about that.'

'You do?' I peered up at my dad and realised, not for the first time, how little I actually knew of him. 'You used to play?'

'Yes . . . All the time when I was a nipper – and I wasn't all that bad either, I'll tell you. I used to be a fast little fella. They called me the dark terrier.' He snorted quietly. 'Of course, it didn't last long. I played less when I started at the factory, although I was still part of their team. But after my accident . . .'

'I'm sorry, Dad,' I said quietly.

'Aw, it's all right. These things happen, I suppose.' He sighed. 'At least I got to show Freddie some tricks or two. I always imagined he'd end up playing for a team, you know.'

'And instead *I* did,' I scoffed. 'Well, not for long anyway. I guess it served me right going and getting injured – what was I even thinking?'

Dad frowned down at me. Acros
screamed as the ball was struck b
and a goal gained. 'What do you me

'I don't know . . .' I shrugged. '
for the shortest time, I believed that I might actually be good at something. I don't know, maybe I would make you proud of me . . .'

Dad's large hand rested on my shoulder, his vice-like grip squeezed tight. 'I've *always* been proud of you, Hettie. I'm proud of all of my children. I'm not good with words and stuff, I know that. I get things wrong. But I've always been proud of you.'

'Really?' My eyes were shining. 'Even now, when the one thing I'm really good at, I can't do any more?'

'That's no fault of yours – I know that better than anyone. We can't help what life throws at us. We can only try and make the best of the hand we are dealt.' He paused, squeezed my shoulder again. 'I was there, you know.'

'Where?'

'At the game. On Christmas Day. I was in the crowd. I stood there as they cheered for your women. I looked down and watched as this team of girls played football just as well as any man I'd ever seen. I realised then that I was wrong, with what I said before. This wasn't a man's

It never had been. It was simply sport, being played t how it should be.'

I reached up and touched his arm. 'Thank you.'

He smiled back. 'And you know – I also saw you that day, standing on the sidelines, cheering your women on. Helping them to succeed. Do you know what I saw then?'

'No,' I whispered.

'My inspiration,' he replied.

He drew his arm tighter around my shoulders. We stood, quite silently, simply watching the boys play, and I wondered if this was what true happiness felt like.

In fact, I didn't wonder.

I knew.

Later, before I retreated to bed, I slipped into Freddie's room to wish him goodnight. He was still sitting upright in his bed, looking around the room. He looked so peaceful and at rest.

'It's quiet here,' he said. 'Even with the street noise and the creaks of the house, it's quiet. There's no screaming. No crying out. No sounds of gunfire—'

His voice broke. I kept quiet. It didn't feel right to speak right then.

'And it's good to be back with you all,' he said. 'I can start again, can't I?'

'Yes, you can.'

I stepped towards him, the box in my hand. It hadn't felt right to give it to him before, but here, in the privacy of this room, I felt it was time.

'Freddie . . . the girls wanted you to have this. It came from the money raised from the matches. As an injured solider, and an ex-Dick, Kerr employee, they felt you should have something more personal.'

'I don't deserve anything,' Freddie said gently. 'I was just doing what every other man did. I was only trying my best.'

'You do deserve it, Freddie. Please.' I handed him the box. 'They will be most offended if you don't accept it. Have you ever seen a bunch of female footballers when they're angry?'

Freddie snorted. 'I'm guessing it's best avoided.'

'And Mr Frankland wanted you to have it, too. In fact, the gift itself was his idea.'

'Alfred, eh? The sly fox.' Freddie considered this for a moment and then carefully opened up the gift. His fingers dug around the loose paper contained inside before finally drawing out the hidden present.

'Oh, my . . .' he said. 'The old devil! I can't believe he did this.'

'What is it, Freddie? I wasn't allowed to look. I've been dying to know.'

Freddie pulled out the gift. In his hand was a beautiful camera. Brand new and shiny.

'That's what he meant!' I said, realising now.

Freddie looked at me, confused. 'Eh?'

'Mr Frankland. He said it was something to help you fulfil your purpose . . . Photography – of course! Because he knew you always wanted to do it. He said the Dick, Kerr Girls wanted you to succeed.'

Freddie nodded. 'Aye. Maybe I can now, with this. It's a really good start, any road.'

'Do you have any idea what you will take pictures of? Nature, maybe? Birds?'

'No, not that,' Freddie said, smiling. 'But do you know, I *do* have a good idea what. I'm going to take pictures of the most wonderful and exciting women I know. Women who are going to change the world. Women who are going to make others stand up and talk.'

'Oh,' I said smiling. 'They sound rather amazing.'

'They really are,' he replied. 'I'm lucky enough to be related to one.'

I stared back at him; suddenly all words were lost to me.

My brother. My Freddie was proud of me!

Freddie settled himself back into his pillow. 'Go back to bed now, Hettie. It's late. We both need rest. Go to bed and dream. Dream of the future – our wonderful, bright new future. Dream it for both of us.'

'I will, Freddie. I will,' I promised.

And I knew it would be brighter than we could possibly imagine.

This was only our beginning.

ABOUT THE AUTHOR

Eve Ainsworth is an award-winning author, creative workshop coordinator and public speaker who draws from her extensive work with teenagers to write authentic, honest and real novels for young people.

Eve is also a passionate football fan and although being born with two left feet, she can often be found on a cold Saturday afternoon cheering on her son from the sidelines.

Eve lives in Crawley, West Sussex with her husband, two young children and slightly crazy dog.

LACE UP YOUR BOOTS AND GET READY FOR KICK OFF – THE NEXT DICK, KERR GIRLS NOVEL IS COMING SOON . . . !